The Keyhole Opera

The Keyhole Opera

Bruce Holland Rogers

Bruce Holland Rogers

🌾 **Wheatland Press**

http://www.wheatlandpress.com

🌾 Wheatland Press

http://www.wheatlandpress.com

P. O. Box 1818
Wilsonville, OR 97070

Copyright © 2005 by Bruce Holland Rogers

Some of these stories first appeared in the following publications:
The North American Review, The Quarterly, New Mexico Humanities Review, Northwest Review, Fourteen Hills, Westword, Realms of Fantasy, Harpur Palate, Talebones, Aeon, The Asylum Annual, The Illinois Review, Portland Review, Abyss & Apex, Horror Garage, Polyphony 1, Polyphony 2, Polyphony 3, Xaxx Quarterly (United Kingdom), *Prairie Dog 13* (United Kingdom), *Descant* (Canada) and *Imago* (Australia).
"Avery's Story," "The Last Unseen Window in the Last Unseen Car," and "Something Like the Sound of Wind in the Trees" were first published in *Quarterly West*.
"Lydia's Orange Bread" first appeared online at the *3 AM Magazine* web site.
"Periwinkles" was first published on the web site of *The Absinthe Literary Review*

Library of Congress Cataloging-in-Publication data is available upon request.
ISBN 0-9755903-7-5
Printed in the United States of America
Cover by Lara Wells.
Interior by Deborah Layne

Contents

An Introduction to an Overture to *The Keyhole Opera* by Michael Bishop

BEAR WITH ME. Few books require two introductions by the same introducer, but this one unaccountably does.

Bruce Holland Rogers, the author of *The Keyhole Opera* (a title deriving from Kate Wilhelm's provocative observation about the contents of an earlier Rogers collection, *Flaming Arrows*, i.e., that the short-short story "offers a glimpse through a keyhole"), well, Bruce believes that although he groks the game I play in my "Overture," which follows, an uninitiated reader may require a primer to get up to speed and to play along.

I concur.

When Bruce asked me to write an introduction to *The Keyhole Opera*, I accepted immediately, but knew that I would defer its authorship owing to a host of other standing obligations. Still, how could I decline? Bruce's stories—freshly conceived, attentively observed, and tenderly crafted—speak to me as do the works of only the very best writers among either my contemporaries or his. (I believe I'm about fourteen years older than he.) But when I sat down to write my introduction, I wanted to pay homage to one of the hardest workers, most unusual talents, and most vivid personalities now committing short fiction. A writer of Bruce's caliber deserves no less.

A glance at the table of contents reveals that Bruce Holland Rogers writes all sorts of compelling stuff. The labels he applies to the fictions in this volume include stories, metamorphoses, insurrections, tales, and symmetrinas, and the monikers of the first four categories strongly suggest their approach and/or subject matter. However, symmetrinas probably gives the new reader pause. What is a symmetrina?

A fixed prose form that Bruce originated and that he writes with great passion and skill. I highly regard all three appearing in

vii

this volume' final section, but view the third, "The Main Design That Shines Through Sky and Earth," as a masterpiece not only of its particular kind, but also of the art of the short story, period. It deserves and repays many readings. The devisers of future fiction-writing texts, I predict, will one day include it in their books as frequently as today's include Ray Bradbury's "And There Will Come Soft Rains," Ernest Hemingway's "Hills Like White Elephants," or Gabriel García Márquez's "A Very Old Man with Enormous Wings."

In any case, I decided that I would frame my introduction as a symmetrina, which always includes an odd number of sections, with the longest in the middle and mirroring sections fore and aft. Section 4 of the Overture, which follows, presumes to explain the process, but the entire Overture presumes to illustrate it. If imitation is the sincerest form of flattery, imitating a form that the flatteree has originated surely elevates the satellite's earnestness to a celestial apogee. Also, like Bruce, I relish the element of play implicit in fulfilling the requirements of a fixed form, right down to limiting each section to an exact number of words. But Bruce thought of it first.

In Section 5, incidentally, the mentors whom "Rattlesnake Hiram Belize" visits correspond to writers whom Bruce admired as a young man or admires even yet. "Mister Ray," an early hero of my own, stands for Ray Bradbury; "Papa" for Ernest Hemingway, another of my youthful idols; and "the Colombian" for Gabriel García Márquez, the great realist magician. In Section 6, "Billy Hitchcock Raintree" represents both Bruce and another of his influences, Richard Brautigan, author of Trout Fishing in America. And Yasunari Kawabata, like García Márquez a Nobel laureate, appears as himself for reasons that I hope he clarifies in that section.

A couple of final matters: In further homage to Bruce, I resolved to write the nine parts of my symmetrical Overture, which follows, using the nine rhetorical modes that instructors of challenging courses in freshman composition present to their students as models. (A writer who strives to make the work harder rather than easier – because difficulty focuses his mind – is one whose impulses vibrate in harmony with my own.) Thus, you will find the nine modes of discourse at play in the Overture, which follows, in this deliberate order: 1) definition, 2) exemplification, 3) description, 4) process analysis, 5) narrative, 6) comparison and contrast, 7) classification and division, 8) cause-and-consequence analysis, and 9) argument. Finally, I dedicate the Overture, which follows, to Bruce Holland Rogers, whose stories have inspired it and whose genius springs from a play ethic as searching as his talent.

Rogerian Modes of Discourse: An Overture

For Bruce Holland Rogers

1. Hello, Hello

I make this overture, reader, to facilitate a relationship – not between you and me, but between you and Bruce Holland Rogers. An overture also generally precedes an opera, however modest or grand.

Modesty, we know, does not preclude profundity.

Listen.

2. Man in a Moving Cage

Listening, you conclude that Rogers inhabits a cage moving through forty many-shafted tunnels. Whenever the cage stops, he kneels before its door (more a fixed panel than a portal) to peer through its keyhole. Each glimpse, you figure, adds to the observations – opuses or opera – carrying his retinal imprints, visions that he meticulously preserves for expectant audiences outside the tunnels.

You take back this conceit, for no one is less likely to inhabit a cage than is Bruce Holland Rogers.

3. Portrait of the Artist

Bruce Holland Rogers boasts seven, nine, or eleven heads — always an odd number. His visions require such oddity. But if a person stares at him face-on, only one head shows. It resembles a melancholy dolphin's, the tentacle of a sea anemone, a lump of tattered rags, a mask made from a dead potter's skin, or the face of a scholar bemused to address the minor poets of a mountain hamlet.

So disguised, Rogers commits blue-sky murders, writes résumés and vocabulary quizzes, flies a kite fabricated from the body of a boy born moribund, and rides in a car as far east as his daddy can drive it. He holds most of his heads aslant this dimension so that only one at a time impinges upon it, and he sneaks up on friends and strangers alike with the air of one who treasures his faceless multiplicity.

When Bruce Holland Rogers confronts a mirror, his reflection echoes forever in the silver-backed glass.

4. How to Write a Symmetrina

Bruce Holland Rogers donned his Shakespeare doublet, his Guy de Maupassant trousers, and his O. Henry moccasins, and padded to the door of his paper house — through which his visitor had poked her fist.

Rogers spied her through the hole, and through other holes that others had poked; and although she had no features but holes for eyes, tinier holes for nostrils, and a slit for a mouth, a sign around her neck said APPRENTICE. He led her inside and gave her a scrap of paper saying APPLE, which she devoured.

"What do you wish to learn?" Rogers asked.

"How to write a symmetrina."

Rogers handed her three specimens of this fixed prose form of his own invention (albeit with some help from friends), then told her to riddle it and explain it aloud. Her brow furrowed.

Finally she said, "Always an odd number of sections."

"Good."

Lustrous irises appeared in her eyeholes. "Each section tells its own story, but all have one theme."

"Excellent."

Her nostrils grew a nose. "One must order the parts in a nice pattern—longest in the middle, shorter ones at the ends."

"Always?"

"Well, mirroring sections always have the same length, down to the word."

Rogers smiled.

Her mouth acquired soft lips. "Two mirroring sections are told by an 'I'; two others focus on 'you'; but all the rest are told like fairy tales, 'he' or 'she' performing."

Rogers nodded. "Bravo, Grace."

Grace had a name! Her eyes and lips glistened; her nose twitched appealingly. "The number of words deciding the part lengths is the maker's. It's doubled, redoubled, and so on until the middle section, when the maker starts back down."

"Impressive, Sherlock."

Palely, Grace spit up a handful of apple—not paper, but fruit pulp. However, she left ecstatic, wearing her new face.

Rogers, meanwhile, found that his own features had vanished. He sat down with pen and ink to rediscover them.

5. Three Enormous Old Men, Possibly Winged

Faceless and untried, a young man longed to make art. He called himself Rattlesnake Hiram Belize, but never aloud, because aliases (except in the salons of his fancy, where he danced like the dust, sang like an ensorcelled lark, and played the piano like an undead Liberace) offended him.

So, after saddling Pertinacity, Hiram rode out of the mountains into a new phase of his life.

On the sidewalks of the City of Angels, no one knew him, and even Pertinacity, who sometimes whickered in quiet alarm, made little impression on the natives. They sidestepped his horse, shoved it in the flank, or rolled their eyes at the plodding slowness of the beast. He wondered at their rudeness, although one kindly guy cautioned him not to leave any horses' durves out on the streets: The mayor would make him skedaddle, pronto.

So Hiram leapt down to buy a whiskbroom and a dustpan at a hardware shop, but wound up gazing at the tomes in a bookstore window. He entered and haled a clerk, who turned upon him a radiant face while scissoring ample silver-white wings: the first angel he'd seen in the alleged City of Angels. He reddened, but could not speak, prompting her to ask what he wanted.

Wings, he mouthed, but no word sounded.

"Ah, you want Mister Ray." She led him through the store and into a cubbyhole where an enormous white-haired man sat at a typewriter typing. Hiram could not have been more surprised if Mister Ray had proved an armor-clad giant roasting venison. The typewriter rattled like a Gatling gun; pages wafted out like heat-bleached leaves.

"What do you want?" Mister Ray asked without looking up.

"The Secret. Power. Wings." Hiram gathered some pages and discovered that however he shuffled them, they told astonishing tales—lyrical, horrific, mad.

"You don't want me, Snakebite. You want Papa."

"How do I find Papa?"

Mister Ray looked up. "Use the Kilimanjaro Machine. Hop in. Take off."

"Where is it? Don't I have to pass a test?"

"You rode in on it. The tests never end."

Hiram rode the Kilimanjaro Machine, his own Pertinacity, to Paris. He arrived after dark at a clean, well-lighted bar where an enormous, white-bearded man stood alone at a lectern scribbling on posterity with an antique pen. Hiram dismounted and entered.

"Welcome, kiddo. What do you want?"

"Are you Papa?"

Papa shrugged.

"But where are your wings, sir?"

"Wings? I prefer work. You?"

"I like yours a lot, but I'd also like wings. A girl in LA—young woman, I mean—hers totally bowled me over."

"You don't want me, kiddo. You want the Colombian."

"How do I find him—via my Kilimanjaro Machine?"

"Absolutely. Fly the steed you rode in on." Papa waved an age-spotted hand, and Pertinacity stepped into the bar like a solemn, wingless Pegasus.

Aboard Pertinacity, Hiram soared back across the Atlantic, to land near a rusty chicken coop behind an adobe hovel. An enormous old man dressed like a rag picker, tiny wings sprouting from his shoulders, hovered over the mud like a swami, beatifically smiling. One finger inscribed curlicues of light on the air while midges swarming from his feathers etched a bleak halo about his head.

"Are you the Colombian?"

"¿Qué quiere?" said a curlicue at the man's fingertip.

"Wings."

"Wings are unnecessary," the finger wrote. "Mire su caballo."

"You have wings!"

"Yes. But I am a saint." The Colombian farted. His handwriting dissolved.

The smell struck Hiram. He spurred Pertinacity skyward, who arose more slowly than Hiram found convenient.

A dark cloud engulfed them. He laid his cheek on the horse's mane and wept as gravity and darkness dragged them back toward earth. Hands—small hands—massaged his neck and kept him from turning about when he tried to.

But her wings held them both aloft.

6. Nightingale Birding in Japan

Billy Hitchcock Raintree published a peculiar little novel, *Nightingale Birding* in Japan. When it sold forty thousand copies, its publisher sent him to the Land of the Rising Sun on a book tour.

Billy wearied of signings and interviews, all with an indefatigable translator. He had never actually done much birding, he loved the word nightingale more than he did the bird, and he'd set his book in Japan rather than Shangri-La because his editor loathed fantasy.

"Take me somewhere quiet," Billy pleaded.

His publicist took him to a Shinto shrine where he meditated amid the mountain bamboo, forgetting *Nightingale Birding* altogether and sewing silken patches on his soul.

One evening, a frail, kimono-clad man introduced himself at dinner by presenting Billy a copy of his novel *The Sound of the Mountain*—a sound that Billy had lately begun to hear.

This was Nobel laureate Yasunari Kawabata, also on retreat.

Miraculously, Kawabata knew Billy's work—not just *Nightingale Birding*, but small-press poems and stories long out of print. He remarked that although Billy and he differed in age, race, nationality, etc., as artists many similarities linked them.

Billy marveled: His subconscious was fulfilling a chimerical wish.

Despite writing novels, Kawabata said, they both preferred the cameo to the panorama, dragonflies to droning bombers. Had Billy been born Nipponese, he would have written haiku; instead, he wrote epigrams rather than epics, tales rather than sagas, and so indisputably qualified as a palmist.

"But I don't read palms."

"A writer of palm-of-the-hand stories," Kawabata said. "A miniaturist."

Ah. Rather than dwindling in his own estimation, Billy enlarged.

At length Kawabata said Sayonara and retired.

Billy noticed that his copy of *The Sound of the Mountain* was in Japanese, which he could not read. Later his publicist revealed that Kawabata, who left that very evening, could not speak English. How, then, had they understood each other?

High on the mountain, a nightingale sang.

7. Q&A

"What sorts of stories do you write?"

"Besides short-shorts and symmetrinas?"

"Yeah."

"Everything in the hallowed five traditions."

"Meaning?"

"True experience, speculation, amusing anecdote, dream narratives, and poetic story."

"Anything else?"

"Metamorphoses, fairy tales, stories illustrating a scientific principle, mysteries, stories that pull a 'faces-into-vase' trick."

"What differences exist between poetic short-shorts and prose poems?"

"In stories, something changes. Lyric poems, whether verse or prose, can remain static."

"Whaddayamean, 'something changes'?"

"A narrative moves us from state A to state Z—or sometimes only to state B."

"Yeah, vignettes. What else?"

"Insurrections."

"What do your 'insurrections' rise up against?"

"The reader's expectations. My insurrections say, No, I won't give you what you expect when you think 'story.' "

"Isn't that mean?"

"You're the sort of person who likes to get to the bottom of stuff, aren't you?"

"Aren't you?"

"I'm the sort of writer who likes to write the sort of story I haven't written lately."

"Okay. Thanks. Sayonara."

8. Fictional Self-Improvement

You want something spiffy and invigorating to read, and you remember that story in *The Sun*, or *Polyphony*, or the online magazine *Flashquake*, and so you order Bruce Holland Rogers's collection *Flaming Arrows*.

You take its twenty-seven off-the-wall arrows right to the heart, and, full of their fiery savor, you order *Thirteen Ways to Water*, an anthology featuring "The Dead Boy at Your Window," and, last but not least, *The Keyhole Opera*.

Result: You get happier and lots, lots smarter.

9. My Closing to the Jury

Bruce Holland Rogers is a one-man story-writing revolution.

Who else emails three stories a month to over 500 subscribers?

Who else has devised a fixed prose-fiction form of the lovely versatility of the symmetrina?

Who else — ?

But I rest my case.

Michael Bishop
Pine Mountain, Georgia
July 27-29, 2005

I. Stories

Avery's Story

I STILL DON'T KNOW ANYTHING about her. I was standing across the street, near the intersection, waiting for a bus. She carried an armload of boxes wrapped with green paper and decorated with red and silver ribbons. But I don't think I noticed those packages. I'm sure I didn't. Not then. I hardly noticed her at all at first.

Maybe a hundred feet from the intersection, she started across the street. The driver must have been trying to beat the yellow. He should have been able to see her in time.

I understood what was about to happen a moment before she did. The instant she knew, I saw it in her eyes. Somehow the distance between us contracted. I could see her face so clearly. It couldn't have taken a second. First, she recognized her peril, and for an instant she thought she would spring away, but her legs betrayed her and in the next moment her eyes—they were gray eyes—in the next moment her eyes filled with resignation and she shifted her gaze slightly beyond the car and onto me. The tires were squealing in that slow half second, and her gaze reached me in time to say, *please*, and I answered, *yes*, and just before she passed from this loneliness into another, neither of us was alone.

The sound—I could hear it beneath the tire squeal—was innocent as a line drive kissing the glove. The Christmas presents bounced off the windshield.

I could have gone to the driver while he knelt beside her with his head in his hands. But the poor bastard was too complicated. I could never give him what I had given her.

3

The Last Unseen Window in the Last Unseen Car

I TAKE IT ALL BACK. NO PHONE call woke me at two in the morning. No stranger's voice told me to be at the train station no later than three fifteen to meet the father I had never known.

It isn't true that I fumbled with my shirt buttons, dressing in the dark, or that my face felt slack with the Novocain of sleep. Did I say I gasped at the shock of January air? Not so.

No cab came for me, and I didn't shiver in the back seat as street light shadows marched forward through the cab, one after another. If the street was particularly dark and particularly still that night, I didn't see it. I wasn't there to see the traffic light flashing yellow or red.

If I ever said that I stood on the platform watching the clouds of my breathing rise toward the stars, forgive me. I am not comfortable with lies. Let me be clear about this: no trains came at all. No freight train with cars that said Chelsea or Rio Grande or Pacific or Burlington Northern thundered by. No Amtrak train rolled by without stopping. Or if it did, I wasn't there for it, didn't stand under the defective platform light that snapped suddenly off, hummed as it turned blue, burned into orange brilliance, and snapped off again one, two, three, four times before the last car rolled by.

If there was a man's shadow, a silhouette, framed in the last window of the last car, I don't know anything about it.

I didn't walk all the way home. I didn't tell myself that it was better this way, that the man I imagined couldn't disappoint me when I could see no trace of myself in him.

No snow crunched beneath my boots.

Lydia's Orange Bread

WASH FOUR ORANGES, UNLESS you have just broken up with Jamil Becker, in which case to hell with washing them. Peel them. Set aside the sections to eat while you're cooking. Put the peels in a sauce pan with one teaspoon of baking soda and enough water to cover. Boil the peels for ten minutes.

Drain, and rinse in cold water. Scrape away the white part of the peel. Cut the orange peel into slivers, unless you have just broken up with Jamil Becker, who has very long eyelashes for a man, dark eyes, and a mouth made—as other women have said about the mouths of other such men—for kissing and lying. In that case, think about the woman you saw him with last weekend and keep cutting the peel until the slivers are reduced to specks and the specks are reduced to mush.

Pre-heat the oven to three hundred and fifty degrees.

Candy the orange peel by boiling in one cup of sugar and one cup of water until reduced to about one third of the original volume. If you're using a candy thermometer, what you want is the hard ball stage, but candy thermometers, like some men, can't always be relied on. One-third of the original volume is a better guide. Trust your eyes.

Set aside the candied peel.

7

Mix two tablespoons of melted butter, two eggs, one cup of sugar and one cup of milk. You can use an electric mixer, but if you have just broken up with Jamil Becker, do this step by hand. Vigorously.

Sift together a pinch of salt, three tablespoons of baking powder, three and one-quarter cups of flour. Add the wet mixture to the dry. If you've broken up with Jamil Becker, pause here to cry, then get angry and tell yourself to get over it already. Remind yourself that baking something complicated always makes you feel better. Add the orange peels and one cup of chopped pecans.

Spoon into two greased bread pans and bake for one hour.

When the loaves have cooled, slice them and you're done, unless you have just broken up with Jamil Becker, who has apparently forgotten that he gave you a set of keys to his apartment. In which case, put the sliced loaves in a paper bag along with four softened sticks of butter, drive to his apartment while he's at work, and let yourself in.

Step over the clothes on the living room floor. Pet the cat.

Go to his closet and take out the cream-colored silk shirt that you bought him for his birthday and lay it on the bed. Butter a slice of orange bread and put it butter-side down on the shirt pocket. Butter some more slices and put one in the breast pocket of each of his suits. Put a slice and an extra pat of butter under his pillow.

Open the drawers of his dresser, leaving a buttered slice under his socks, under his undershorts. Close the drawers. Hide a slice inside a lampshade, where the light will warm it and melt the butter onto the bulb.

Open the sealed but un-mailed letter on his kitchen table, addressed to his college buddy, Randy. Read the sentence where Jamil complains about his girlfriend. Re-read it to be sure he means you. Find a pen, scratch out the word "paranoid" and write above it the word, "prescient." Scratch out "a little spooky" and write above it "dangerous." Put the letter back into the envelope, along with the

8

The Keyhole Opera

apartment keys. Put the envelope inside your purse to mail on your way home.

Leave buttered slices between CD cases, behind the refrigerator, in the fireplace, on top of the television. Make a butter sandwich with two slices and push it into the slot of the VCR.

Pet the cat again. Mash orange bread and butter into many little balls and put them in her food dish. Watch her gulp these down too fast. She won't be able to keep them down for long. Carry her to the sofa and pet her until she's good and settled there.

On your way out, collect your iron and your blender, which he had said he would return. Remember that he had also said, "Lydia, I wouldn't *look* at another woman," which was your first clue because what man can honestly say he wouldn't even look?

One last time before you leave, pet the cat. Her tongue is sticking out a little. She doesn't look good, but she'll feel better soon. You both will.

Stallion

BEFORE CALDERON WALKED HOME to his own ranch, he drank coffee. A lot of coffee. He could tell Palmer's wife wanted him gone. She was moving things on the stove that didn't need moving. But he was tired and kept asking for another cup. He drank the pot dry, and then regretted it because that would be the end. Now he'd really have to go.

Palmer sat across from him at the table, staring out the window past Calderon's shoulder. Toward the corrals. Maybe Palmer was thinking about the stallion, and maybe he was only looking that direction because he was too tired to look anywhere else. The sun was going down, shining in Palmer's face.

Without shifting his gaze, Palmer said, "You want some more?" Meaning coffee, Calderon supposed. He said some more would be nice, but they had drunk the last. Palmer had no answer for that. He just kept looking out the window.

The stallion had never shown any sign of tiring. It threw them just as hard in the afternoon as it had in the morning. The way things looked to Calderon, the horse might break them before they could break it. And maybe that was good. Maybe once in your life, it was good to find a horse you couldn't break.

11

Palmer wouldn't feel that way, of course. He had paid money for the stallion.

Mrs. Palmer came to collect the coffee pot. She put it in the sink and filled it with water. She left it there. Then she went back to moving things around in the kitchen.

Ordinarily they wouldn't have quit until it was too dark to go on, but that horse had taken it out of them. They'd stopped when there was still a good hour and a half of light.

Calderon had heard stories about a certain kind of horse, a horse that might break eventually but would kill a man first. In those stories, the horse always had something wild in its eyes, something that people remarked when they saw it.

This stallion wasn't like that. He'd let you touch his neck and flanks, let you saddle him. There wasn't any madness in his eyes, or meanness. He just knew he wasn't for riding, and he didn't care to be convinced otherwise. After he'd throw you, he'd look at you like he was sorry that you couldn't get such a simple thing into your head.

Palmer's wife got fed up and went to another part of the house. Palmer hadn't moved.

The room was getting dark. It would be a long walk home in the night, Calderon thought, and there would be no moon. He really ought to get up and go, he really should. The longer he sat here the more he felt every bruise, every ache in his bones.

"I ought to shoot that damn horse," Palmer said.

"Sell him."

"Can't. I have a conscience."

Calderon didn't answer. In a moment he would get up. He would. He would stand and walk away from the pleasure of sitting in the dark and aching and thinking of a horse that wouldn't be broken.

He could buy the horse himself, but that would be a waste. It would be money spent to hold on to something that can't be held.

Not in the ordinary sense, anyway.

Outside, the crickets were starting up. "Well," he said, taking his leave, and as he pushed back from the table, Palmer asked him, "Tomorrow?"

Calderon stood up, went to the door. He heard the stallion nicker. The first stars burned. "Be just the same tomorrow," he said, letting the words take whichever shape they would.

And he stepped outside to inhale the cooling, horse-scented air.

As Far East

I OWE IT TO MY FATHER TO BEGIN this story with the real ending, the part that comes after I've told what I want to tell. He'd insist on it because — notwithstanding the opinions of his creditors — he was a realist.

So I'll say right now that this story ends in three days of May rain, the heaviest rain in northern Colorado that year. It ends with everything we had — the old furniture, the encyclopedia samples, my mother's dresses and my father's two suits, my sister's stuffed animals and my Hardy Boys books — everything, soaking on the sidewalk where the Larimer County Sheriff's deputy and our landlord had stacked it days before. There were new tenants in the house already, and my father used their phone to call a friend who owned a truck.

This wasn't the first time we were put out, but it was the first time we weren't there to see it happen. I felt cheated.

The story begins with the night my father shook me awake in the dark and told me to get dressed. The hall light was yellow and wincingly bright behind him, and the sky outside my window was black. That's how it was going to be every day of our journey, getting up before there was any hint of morning. My mother, my sister and I were always dull and slow when we woke up, and

15

that's what my father counted on, getting us on our feet and out the door before we were awake enough to ask questions.

By the time I was really awake, we were passing through a town called Ault. I rolled my window down. When we halted for a stop light that was still flashing red, I could hear the wind moving through the dark leaves of a cottonwood tree. My sister slept in the seat beside me.

My mother said, "Where are we going?"

My father just pointed through the windshield. Ahead of us the sky was beginning to gray.

She said, "Will we be back in time for you to open?"

"Indoor putt-putt was a pretty stupid idea. Don't you think it was a stupid idea?"

"It was fun," I told him, but he wasn't talking to me.

"It's a good idea," my mother said. "One of your best."

"One of my best." He shook his head.

"It got you the loan, didn't it?"

"So this time it's not just our own money I'm losing."

"You keep saying business will turn around."

"That's what I keep saying."

He drove in silence for a while. We were going fast again, and the wind in my face was cold enough to make me shiver.

"We're running away," my mother said, extra-serious, making it a joke.

My father said, "We are not."

"Then where are we going?"

"East," he said. "Sunrise."

I watched the stars fade. Fields of irrigation pipe and just-sprouted corn gave way to sage and grassland.

"Here it comes," my father said when the first bright sliver of sun broke the horizon. We passed Briggsdale about then—a gas station with a rusty Drink Coca-Cola sign. I craned my neck to see, but it was only after we'd gone by that I realized he didn't mean the

16

town.

"This is the best time," my father said. "Milk truck time. Seeing night turn to day makes the rest of the day yours, like a secret."

I woke my sister up then. I said, "You're missing it."

She kicked me and said she was cold. I rolled the window up and shook her again. "Come on," I said, but already the light was different.

When she finally did sit up, she said, "I'm hungry."

"Breakfast soon," my father promised, and then he said, "Maybe I'll drive a milk truck again."

In an hour, we stopped at a McDonald's in Sterling, but it was only to use the bathrooms. There in the parking lot, my father opened the trunk. It was full of brown paper bags. Some of the bags held groceries and the rest were full of folded clothes. My father handed a box of crackers to my sister. "Share them," he said. She hugged the box and grinned at me.

My mother was looking at the clothes.

"Just a vacation," my father told her.

"The kids have school Monday."

"This is more important."

"More important than school?" She looked worried.

"Don't ask me to explain. It will ruin it."

"How are we going to pay for this?"

"There's room enough on the charge cards."

"That doesn't answer the question."

"Let's not worry about it. Facing the music comes later." He searched through another bag. "Who wants an apple?"

After we were back on the road, driving again into the rising sun, my sister paused between crackers to ask, "Where are we going?"

"East," I told her.

"That's not a where," she said.

"No," I admitted.

"Mom," she said, "where are we going?"

My mother didn't answer. Instead, she looked at my father.

"Your brother's right," he said. "We are going east."

"But where?"

"To an eastern place," I said. "Let me have a cracker."

She pulled the box out of my reach.

"You know," my father said, "there's never going to be another trip like this one."

That got her interest. "Why not?"

"This is a mystery trip."

"What's the mystery?" I asked.

"That's also a mystery," my father said. I could see only his eyes in the mirror, but it looked like he was smiling. "The first part of this mystery is figuring out what the mystery is."

"The mystery is where we're going," my sister said.

"Partly," my father said. He looked at my mother. "That's the obvious part. Where are we going?"

"Nebraska," my mother said.

Even though we were passing the Nebraska welcome sign, I didn't think that was the answer.

We had lunch at a park in Grand Island—peanut butter and jelly sandwiches and warm sodas. My father opened the road atlas and studied it there on the picnic table. On the way back to the highway he stopped to buy us ice cream, paying with coins from a mayonnaise jar that he'd kept under the front seat.

He started talking to my mother about why Putt A Round hadn't worked out. "Not leasing something closer to the college was a mistake. Maybe I should have cut and run right away," he said. "Even handing out free passes, we weren't getting anyone in to play."

That wasn't entirely true. My friends and I played the nine

holes after school every day for a month, but we had played about as much putt-putt as we wanted to by the time my father started charging.

He had made the course himself. My father was good with his hands, and he had imagination. All the holes were mechanized. My favorite one had the ramp leading up to a tank turret. The turret rotated, and you had to time your shot so that the gun barrel was pointing at the hole when your ball rolled out.

"Location's the key," my father said, "and I knew that going in. I knew that."

"The rents were too high close to the campus," my mother reminded him. "It would have been worse that way."

"How could it be worse?"

"I mean we would have been broke faster."

"That's true. We've been broke a lot faster than this."

They got to talking about which of my father's businesses had gone broke the fastest, and then because they weren't sure they could remember them all, they started counting backwards from the Putt A Round to the aquarium store to the slot car track.

To keep the order straight, they remembered all the jobs my father had held between business ventures. He had read water meters, driven a snowplow and painted houses. My father had sold shoes, sold soap, sold encyclopedias, and sold vacuum cleaners. He had taken tickets at the college basketball games, installed carpet, tended bar, driven a forklift, delivered phone books and distributed snack foods, sometimes holding two or three jobs at once. He'd never been fired, but nothing interesting ever happened when he was working for someone else. Whenever he quit, we'd have a family party with cake and ice cream.

We left the Interstate and continued east on a two-lane highway. After we crossed the Missouri River, we were in Iowa, but not for long. Another Interstate took us down toward Kansas City. By then my parents were talking about the wooden circus trains my

19

father had made and sold — or tried to sell — before I was born.

Watching the sun, I said, "We're not going east."

He looked at me in the mirror but said nothing. I had interrupted. My mother was talking about the first circus animals he had cut out with the jigsaw. They all looked the same. "Like elephants without a trunk," she said.

My parents laughed. The older the memory, the more likely they were to laugh about it.

"We're going south."

This time, he answered me. "South on the map," he said. "But still east. On this trip, we don't go anywhere but east."

At Kansas City, we changed highways, twisting and turning on the interchanges until the late afternoon sun was right behind us.

We spent that first night at a motel in Saint Charles, Missouri. My father got two rooms, and my mother hardly argued about it. In our room, I let my sister choose what to watch on TV. I wanted to think about the mystery. Where were we going? The only clues I had were where we had been.

The second morning, we started out the again with a black sky over our heads. My sister complained about the cold, but she didn't sleep in the car this time. She saw the stars fade out and the sun rise over Illinois like I did, like we all did.

"Did we ever live in Illinois?" my sister asked.

Illinois, my mother told her, was the only state in the country where we had not, at some time, lived and gone broke.

"That's not quite true," said my father.

After another breakfast of crackers and apples, I asked for the road atlas. Illinois and Indiana were a lot skinnier than the states we had already been through. I traced the line of the Interstate and predicted that we would eat lunch in Kentucky.

My father bought us a McDonald's lunch in Lexington to both fulfill and celebrate my prediction. I ate with the atlas before me.

"We're going to Virginia!" I announced through a mouthful of hamburger.

"Through Virginia," my father said. "Yes."

"Did he solve the mystery?" my sister asked.

"No." He smiled. "No, he did not."

I looked to see where the smaller highways went after the Interstate ended. "North Carolina, then." It was a state I'd never been to.

"You're right," my father said, "that's the last place. But that still doesn't solve the mystery."

"I don't get it," I said.

My sister sighed dramatically and explained, "We are going east."

We spent the second night in a motel in Richmond, and we had another early start the next morning. The sun came up as we drove over a long bridge, and my father said, "That's the Chesapeake Bay."

"I could get a job," my mother told him. "The kids are old enough."

"If it's what you want," he said. Then, on the other side of the bridge, he added, "We'll get back on our feet."

"I know."

"And then I'll have another idea." He laughed.

"I know." There was something strange in her voice, not exactly sad.

"It might be the right idea, the next one I have. It might be something people want, something that makes them happy."

"Anyway, it will sound right," my mother said. "It will sound like heaven on earth at a dollar a head."

After a minute, he said, "Are you sorry?"

"Sometimes," she said.

"So am I," he said. "At the end like this, every time, it's like

21

somebody died."

They didn't say anything else for the rest of Virginia. When we crossed into North Carolina, I felt sad and excited at the same time. It was like getting evicted, wondering what would come next.

We stopped before the sun was halfway up the eastern sky.

"Elizabeth City, North Carolina," my father said.

"Is this where we're going?" my sister asked.

"This is just where we're stopping for the day."

I said, "Why?"

My father didn't answer, so I said in a fake spooky voice, "It's a myst-er-y." That made him laugh.

We went to a museum that had Indian arrowheads and a room full of wooden ducks. When my mother explained what a decoy was for, my sister refused to believe that real ducks could be that stupid.

After lunch, we played miniature golf on a course that wasn't half as good as my father's. Nothing moved. But my father pointed out that it was just off the highway in a tourist town.

The rest of the day, my sister and I goofed around in the pool at the Holiday Inn, the best motel so far.

The last morning was like the others, except that we ate breakfast in our room before we started. The sky was still dark when we drove over the long bridge out of town, and then we were on a ribbon of island with sand dunes on either side of the highway. We stopped twice for my father to consult the atlas, and a salty wind rolled through the open windows of the car. Finally he followed a sign for beach parking and drove to where we could see the ocean. By then, the sky was orange.

"From here, we walk."

We got out. My sister ran ahead and got her shoes wet before anyone could tell her not to. My father took his shoes off and rolled his pants up to his knees. My mother looked at me and shrugged. We took our shoes off, too, and then my father waded calf-deep into the waves.

"This is as far as we can come," he said. "As far east."

I said, "What about Maine?" and my mother said, "Hush."

"No," my father said. "He's right about Maine."

It made me happy to be right, but I was even happier to be standing in the ocean, watching the sun come up. Three days in the car was a long time. It was worth it.

We watched the sunlight on the waves. High above the glimmer, sea gulls rode the wind. My father stared out over the Atlantic as if he were looking for something, but there wasn't anything to see besides the birds, the sun, and the hazy line between sea and sky. The wind was blowing his hair back from his face.

My sister was busy poking something in the water with a stick, so she missed what happened next. Maybe it doesn't matter. Maybe whatever she had found in the water was just as important.

Whatever you remember, that's the thing that matters. That's the thing you get to keep.

Anyway, it was a small thing.

It was this. My father put one hand on my mother's hip and rested the other hand on the back of my neck. The wind was cold, and his hand felt very warm. We stood there for a long time, and even after he had taken his hand away, I could still feel it there. Even after I was alone looking as far east as I could see, after my parents and sister were halfway back to the car, I could feel the warmth of his hand.

Valentine

INSIDE THE SHOPPING MALL, he stood near the entrance to a clothes store. He thought it was the sort of place where his ex-wife would have shopped when they were married. It probably wasn't the sort of place where she bought clothes now. The shoppers going in were all much younger than he was, than his ex-wife was. Probably she dressed very differently these days. He wouldn't know. He hadn't seen her in years.

He held a red envelope.

The way he had imagined it, he would give the valentine to one of the women who was as young as his wife had been back then. But he had already let two such women walk past. They could have been his daughters, if he'd had children.

So he stopped a woman closer to his own age. She was shorter than he would have liked. Heavier. Her lipstick was too red. But he was already launched. "Listen, I know this will seem a little strange, but there's someone I wanted to give a valentine to, only I can't." He was talking too fast. "If I could give it to you..."

"Why?" She looked him in the eye. Her eyes were brown and serious. "Why can't you give it to her yourself?"

"No, I'm not asking you to deliver it or anything. Just to take it. To accept it as a gesture."

She frowned. "What kind of gesture is that? She doesn't even know about it."

"I don't want her to know about it. I mean, I do, but she wouldn't understand. I was married to her a long time ago. She lives in another state. But the way things turned out, I wouldn't want her to think I was asking for anything or expecting anything or..."

"Then what's the point of the valentine?"

"See, that's it. I want to send it to her twenty years ago. I want to send it to her, to who she was, just after we were divorced."

"Divorced," she said. She shook her head. "You're a coward."

"No," he said, though perhaps he was. He had thought of sending the card unsigned, anonymously. He didn't because of the postmark, and because her lover, the man she'd had the affair with, had done things like that, had sent unsigned notes, left flowers on the windshield of her car. Once or twice, he had found these things meant for her. "If I actually sent it to her...she wouldn't know what it meant."

"What's the point of giving it to me, then?"

"We were so young, and I..." He stopped. Her gaze was unrelenting. He couldn't tell this woman, this stranger, about what had happened, about how marriage had been something that he sort of slept through. How, after the papers were all signed, she had made dinner for him. How one thing led to another on the couch, in the bedroom. How she had surprised him, how different she was as a woman than she had been as a wife. He woke up. Making love to her for the last time, when it was too late, he woke up. "My whole life has been different. Better. I'm grateful."

The woman narrowed her eyes. Enunciating, as if to a slow child, she said, "Write her a letter."

He waved the red envelope. "But the valentine..."

She snatched the envelope out of his hand. "All right," she said, raising her voice. Other shoppers turned their heads. "I took the valentine." Hands shaking, she stuffed it into her purse. "Now you're under an obligation. Now you have to write her a letter."

"I never said anything about writing her a letter!" His hands shook, too.

"No, you didn't. But you've got to do it now. And you're going to, aren't you. Aren't you!"

"Give it back to me," he said.

"It's mine now."

He reached.

"You touch my purse..."

"Damn it," he said. "I don't have to write her a letter."

"You do, though." She patted her purse. "You know you do."

Again, he said, "Damn it." But he could hear the difference in his own voice, as if he were admitting something. She nodded. She stepped past him. He watched her walk away, holding the purse close to her body, clutching it as if it contained not an anonymous valentine, but a letter from someone she once loved.

The Burlington Northern Southbound

HER NAME WAS CHRISTINE. He didn't know how to talk to her, so he wrote her a poem in which he compared her to the Burlington Northern southbound out of Fort Collins. He told her about the way he used to stand on the tracks in the dazzle of the headlight. He liked to step aside and stand on the tie edge to feel the thunder in his bones. Between the quaking of the cinders and his joy, the engine would almost bring him to his knees. The diesel throb in his guts would ebb until it was only sound, and then the cars—some shrieking on their springs—would *clataclat clataclat* on by. He'd choose one car, and at a trot he would swing aboard the ladder. He'd feel the night air in his hair, and the cars nearest him would have a music all their own, a rhythm he could never hear if he only stood near the track as each one passed. The horn would sound for the last intersection, a song sweet as jazz. Then, from even fifty cars away, he would feel the vibration of the engine digging in. He would dream for a moment of hanging on, of riding the coupling platform through the night, riding for weary hours in a white-knuckled crouch until the daylight would show him the red hills of New Mexico and the smell of juniper would be in the air. Then he'd leave the dream to notice how fast the ties were flying beneath him. He'd lean out into the wind at the edge of town, and he'd launch himself into the void and land running with a jar we would feel all the way up his spine, a shock he would sense as a flash of white and the taste of electricity, and he'd run and run blindly and sometimes stumble in the cinders and scrape his knuckles and bang his knee. When he could stop at last he'd hear the blood rushing in his ears for a long time while he felt the train rush on and recede, and he'd watch the stars wheel awhile and when he walked home there'd be a ringing in his ears, but gently.

He tried to put this in the poem. It was four pages long and ended:

> I want to ride you home, Christine,
> and beyond. I want to ride you into
> mornings sharp and cold and blue
> and never run the same track twice.

He never heard a word from her, not even to acknowledge that she had received the poem. What woman wants to hear she is like the Burlington Northern southbound?

The Goblin King

WHEN I WAS SMALL, MY FATHER would read me bedtime stories, and my mother would say from another room, "You aren't reading him that poem, are you?"

"It's his favorite before bed!" my father would answer with a wink to me.

I wasn't sure why my father thought the poem about the Goblin King was my favorite. Every night after he read it I would lie awake for a long time, listening to the darkness. Later, I often woke up crying, and my mother would come and hold me. Nevertheless, every night after my last story, my father opened the book of children's poems and quietly read the lines about the Goblin King's spies:

> The Moon is an eye for the Goblin King
> And watches all you do.
> When you pout or cry or shout or whine,
> The spiders tell on you....

Most of the poem was devoted to children who misbehaved and what happened to them when the Goblin King found out. One little boy disappeared up a chimney, snatched by a nameless black thing. A little girl was dragged into a well. And then there was Annie.

> Little Annie was a noisy child,
>> At dinner she banged her plate.
> Her parents sent her to her bed.
>> Alas! They sealed her fate.

> The Goblin King has feet of sand
>> And never makes a sound.
> When Mother pulled the covers back,
>> Here is all she found:

> A shriveled, blackened ball of hair,
>> A tooth, a nail, a bone.
> Nothing more of Ann was left
>> Except, perhaps, a moan.

There was a picture of the Goblin King in the book. He sat on his forest throne, grinning. Except for his yellow teeth and eyes, he was made of forest things—branches, grass, sand, mud, and dried leaves. It was hard to see where the forest ended and the Goblin King began.

One night, the electricity went out in our neighborhood just before my bedtime. I was already in my pajamas, and my father carried me into my bedroom. There was no light for a story, but my father recited from memory:

> The Moon is an eye for the Goblin King
>> And watches all you do.
> When you pout or cry or shout or whine,
>> The spiders tell on you....

The moon had risen outside my window. In the dim light, all I could see were the whites of my father's eyes and the flashing of his teeth.

When Mother pulled the covers back,
Here is all she found:

As he recited, my father grinned a wider and wider grin. His teeth took on a light of their own, and his eyes grew huge. The rest of his body faded away until I couldn't tell where the darkness ended and my father began.

He finished reciting, then tousled my hair and said what he always said before he left me alone with the poem's words still hanging in the black air.

"Be good," he told me. "Be very, very good."

Aftermath

JUSTINE CAME INTO THE dining room, cupping her hand beneath a spoon that dripped yellow sauce. "I'm glad you didn't have to work late. Aren't those flowers great? Four dollars for a bouquet, can you believe it? And I found a bottle of that Petite Syrah that you liked. Take your coat off, dear. Did you wind the clock?"

Howard did not look up from the newspaper. His car keys lay on the tablecloth next to his crystal wineglass. "Later," he said.

"Please? You already read the paper at breakfast."

He looked up. "Watch the spoon. You're going to stain the carpet." It was a cream-colored carpet.

Justine looked at the spoon as if she were surprised to see it in her hand, but what she said was, "It chimed seven. Didn't you hear how slow it was?"

"You just dribbled."

She looked at her feet. "I caught it." She showed him her cupped hand. "See? You're going to love dinner. Now would you wind the clock?"

He took in a deep breath, then exhaled loudly. "All right." He closed the paper. The headline read, "Death Toll Rises."

After she had gone back into the kitchen, he read the headline story again. Then he stood and put his car keys in his pocket where

35

they belonged. Everything in its place, whether it mattered or not. He went into the living room. He took the clock key from its drawer, then went to the mantel where the clock sat among ballerina figurines. He opened the crystal. As he fitted the key into the clock, his hand trembled. He hesitated. He took another deep breath, let it out slowly, and without winding the clock put the key down.

Howard looked toward the kitchen, bit his lip, then took the clock from the mantel and brought it over to the oak secretary where he opened a drawer and found a paperclip. He unbent the clip, then hooked it over the balance wheel. The clock stopped ticking. He replaced it on the mantel and wound it.

He returned to the table just as Justine carried in their salad bowls. "Did you wind it?" she asked.

"Didn't I say I would?"

She put the bowls down and turned back toward the kitchen. "I'm fussing, I know. The house just doesn't feel right to me without that clock chiming the quarter hours."

Howard folded his newspaper, and after she had again left the room he said, "I know."

She came back in with their dinner plates loaded with steak and pilaf and asparagus drizzled with the yellow sauce. The steaks were garnished with a lemon slice and a sprig of rosemary. "How was your day? Mine was marvelous. Business was slow all over the store, but I had three big ring-ups. Bianca said it's all about attitude."

He took up his fork and knife. He cut his meat.

"So how was your day?"

"My day." He shook his head.

"Not so good? Tomorrow will be better."

"I'm not counting on it."

"Well, your job has always given you a great deal of satis —"

"It's not about my job," he said. He nodded at the paper.

She followed his gaze. "You can't let that get you down."

"Can't I?"

She twisted her napkin in her hands. "It doesn't have to touch us."

"It's better if it does touch us. It's touching everyone."

If the clock had been running, it would have struck the quarter-hour by now.

He said, "There are times when it is obscene to be cheery. Obscene!"

Justine's face was white. She threw her wadded napkin onto her plate. She knocked her chair over in her hurry to stand and leave. He heard her feet on the stairs, heard the bedroom door close. If she cried, she did so too softly for him to hear.

Later, he would take the clip out of the balance wheel and set the clock to chiming again. Later, after she had been miserable for a while.

His hands trembled again as he worked the fork and knife—cutting, biting, chewing. He was miserable, too, but felt the satisfaction of misery that was, at least, the right thing to feel.

The Minor Poets of San Miguel County

IT WAS MORE FLYING THAN he had done for years, from Urbana to Chicago, Chicago to Denver, and then from Denver over the mountains to Montrose on a little plane that shook and bumped and left him feeling his age. Not that it took much to make him feel his age. Not since his wife died. He picked up the rental car, then checked his watch and the map again. The letter had told him to pick up a key at the library in Telluride by six. If he drove the speed limit—and he had no intention of driving any faster than that—he would just make it. There was no provision for what he might do if he happened to arrive late.

His calculations did not allow for cattle on the highway, but twenty minutes into his drive, he joined a line of cars waiting behind a state patrol car as the officer and a few bystanders waved their hats and yelled, herding a dozen brown and white Herefords onto the shoulder and down toward the river, back through an open gate. The delay was only ten minutes, but it was ten minutes that he'd have to make up. He calculated how much faster he would have to go, pushed the speedometer needle higher, and then a little higher as he realized that the speed limit would likely drop once he drove into the canyons.

By the time he passed the first ski condominiums, it was twenty past six.

The town wasn't much. Four or five streets paralleled the canyon with perhaps a dozen cross streets. The library was easy to find. He tried the doors. Locked. No movement inside. He rapped on the glass.

"Hey!" called a voice from across the street. "You the professor?" A man wearing an apron stood in front of a restaurant's open doors and invited him to use the restaurant phone. There was no answer the first two times he called. When he did reach the librarian, she asked if he wouldn't mind showing himself to the house where he'd be staying. The key would be on the lintel.

The house, a small Victorian gingerbread painted green and yellow, perched on a steep side street. Inside, shelves made of weathered wood were decorated with old books and rusted tools. Floorboards creaked as he explored the two bedrooms with cast iron beds and gingham down comforters. Hand-lettered signs in the kitchen and bathroom cautioned that the plumbing was delicate. Decaying, in other words. He returned to the front room where he now noticed a tilt to the floor. Year by year, this house and the houses around it were creeping downhill. Year by year, everything dies or falls down.

Beyond the wavy glass of the front window, at the head of the canyon, bare massifs of granite and melting snow towered in the east. Tomorrow they would block the morning sun.

What was he doing here? A man or woman with a whole career to look forward to could make better use of this honor. Such as it was. Speaking to the Poetry Guild of San Miguel County would hardly be the featured event on anyone's curriculum vitae.

Months ago, as he sat reading in his living room, the president of the Guild had called him. Her frail and ancient voice faded in and out as she seemed to forget now and then that she was holding the phone. Would he come to Colorado to give a talk about Rilke?

Based on his paper?

What paper could she mean? He had specialized in Soviet poetry, mostly, with some forays into Polish and Czech. He'd written on Spanish poets, too, and Romanian. He hardly read any German at all. Then he remembered the piece. He'd written it graduate school. What was the name of the little Princeton journal that had published it?

"That was a long time ago," he said. "I'm retired."

"We've all read it," she told him. "I made copies. I hope that was all right. Should I have written to the publisher first?" Her last words faded as she spoke them. She said something else he couldn't hear.

"I'm flattered," he said. He wondered if he would even have a copy of that paper anywhere. "But I'm afraid —"

"We have a grant for the airplane ticket," she said. "We can bring in one speaker, and we voted. May I say that you're..." The last word was inaudible.

He looked at the base of his phone, as if he would find a volume control there, and his gaze happened to fall on his wife's portrait. He hadn't been out of the house much lately, and not out of town for a long time. Magda had always insisted that they travel in the summer. *What will we do here?* she would say. *Watch the corn grow?*

"All right," he heard himself say to the caller. "I'll come."

He hadn't been able to find a copy of the journal, but his files held a yellowed manuscript of the paper. It wasn't structured very well, and the thesis was superficial and vague.

Now in the front room of the house in Telluride, he took out the manuscript and read it again. Carrying it halfway across the country hadn't improved it. As a young man, he had been a muddled, over-emotional thinker. Yet this was what they wanted from him tomorrow, not something more disciplined and mature.

He opened the book of Rilke translations and made some notes.

41

He drew up a better outline of the paper's points and recopied this in large letters that he could read at the podium. It was dark by the time he had finished.

He walked back down to the main street and had dinner at a noisy bar, apparently the only choice open. He drank three beers, which he regretted as he walked back up the hill to his temporary home. His heart hammered. He had to stop twice to rest. At this altitude, one beer would have been too much. Before bed, he drank as much water as he could stand to drink. Then he was waking up all through the night, negotiating the sloping floor to the bathroom.

Morning found him bleary eyed, but mercifully not hung over.

At nine, he walked to the library, where the Guild president — white-haired, palsied and dressed for church — pressed into his hands a poorly reproduced chapbook of her doggerel. One by one, she introduced him to the members. They were ranch wives, mechanics, waitresses, carpenters. By nine thirty-five he was at his place at the podium. Arrayed before him were members and guests of the Poetry Guild of San Miguel County. The president sat alone in the front row. Behind her sat a young man in grease stained blue jeans. Next to him, a girl with a silver stud in her nose waited with a purple pen poised over her notebook. A man in a cowboy hat leaned against the back wall, arms crossed. About thirty people in all, mostly too young to have anything worth writing a poem about. As Rilke himself had observed, writing poetry in one's youth was a waste. Only at an advanced age might one manage ten good lines.

So here he was, before what he now thought of as The Minor Poets of San Miguel County. Of course. What else should he have expected? A better paper would have gone right over their heads. In fact, his youthful gush over Rilke was probably just right.

He hadn't known he was tense until he felt his shoulders relax. He looked at his notes, looked up, and began. Many of Rilke's best poems, he said, depended on a concrete main image that flowered into revelation with the last lines. In this way, their movement was a bit like Shakespearean sonnets.

He read some examples. The meticulously washed corpse that in the last lines, "gives commands." The light pouring from the statue of Apollo, telling us that we must change our lives. And as he spoke, he felt himself standing a little straighter.

"Rilke helps us to see his subject," he said, "and then twists our perspective. He gives us the image, then hints at its meaning. But it's never a simplistic or over-determined meaning. He gives us little mysteries to contemplate. The flamingo poem, for example, turns on a single word."

He read the flamingo poem. In the last line, the birds "stride into their imaginary world."

"Why 'imaginary'? There's a reversal here, the exotic birds and their ordinary zoo enclosure. Because they are in a zoo, the flamingos could be striding into the natural world that they remember and imagine. But I think that the imaginary world of the poem has more to do with the power of our imaginations, startled into action by the sight of these improbable birds."

He read the poem about the woman going blind, walking as if some obstacle were always before her, an obstacle that she might overcome, at which time "she would be beyond all walking, and would fly." Into the terror of going blind, the poet admits a spiritual dimension. But not a spiritual dimension that transcends the physical realm. It is the spiritual dimension of the physical, closely observed.

He put aside his notes, opened the book of poems, and read some more examples, letting them speak for themselves. "Let me conclude with this. The technique of observing the world and teasing out a revelation is a great technique for writing memorable poems. But if all we learn from reading Rilke is to write like Rilke, then we're missing his point." He paused. He had more notes, but he might end right there. The man in the cowboy hat was smiling. He, at least, understood. And for those who didn't, perhaps it was

43

best to leave them with a little mystery, something to keep them thinking, something to get them to read the poems for themselves. He said, "Thank you."

In the questions and answers, no one said, "Then what *is* the point?" And they didn't ask at lunch, either, when he ate an elk steak at a restaurant with the Guild officers and any members who cared to come along.

After lunch, the Guild president thanked him, shook his hand, and gave him an envelope with his honorarium. "That was just the talk I was hoping for," she said. "These younger poets need to have a better idea of what poetry is." She offered to walk him back to the house. He declined. He didn't say so, but he thought that the walk up the hill might kill her.

The girl with the silver nose stud and the purple pen was waiting for him when he crossed the street. She wanted him to look at one of her poems.

"My area's not really creative writing," he said, hoping to deter her.

She took this as his modest assent. "The lobby of the Sheridan would be quiet," she said. He found himself following her there, then sat across from her in one of the overstuffed chairs as she rummaged in her knapsack for her poem. Her fingernails were bitten short; her clothes, self-consciously tattered but clean. Her round face was still a girl's more than a woman's.

It was a love poem, short lines of a single verse paragraph running down the center of three pages. No address. She said she hadn't gotten as far as sending her poems out. The metaphor for her lover, for what she wanted from her lover and what she wanted to be for her lover, kept shifting every few lines. A sparrow. Sunlight on sheets. The smell of grass. Wet moss. Split wood. A stone hidden in the earth.

The poem lacked strategy. Its transitions were abrupt. The metaphors, rather than building, were just piled up, one expression of her deepest feelings after another.

He looked at her, met her wide eyes, and had to look away, the poem had made her so beautiful.

"It's..." He thought of the young man she had been sitting next to. "Whoever you wrote this for should feel honored."

She smiled, revealing nothing. "But is it good?"

He took a breath, considered. "Aesthetics are at least partly a matter of fashion," he said. Then he pointed out the things that would probably keep the poem from being published anywhere important.

"So it sucks."

He grimaced. "It doesn't...suck. You have some things to learn, yes. But it's an authentic poem. It really comes out of who you are. That may be the most important thing about a poem."

"I should keep writing?"

You should keep living, he wanted to say. But what he did say was, "That's entirely up to you, my dear."

When she had gone, it was still early afternoon. He didn't feel like returning alone to the little house, so he left his book and notes in the care of the hotel clerk and went to walk along the river, upstream. The path took him out of town, then joined the road to take him past a working mine. The road became stony and steep. He stopped at a switchback to rest, to look at the town below, at the mountain peaks and waterfall above.

At his feet, mountain dandelions flowered profusely, hurrying to set their seed in the short season. The air smelled of beeswax. He didn't know why. He sniffed the white blossoms of some shrubs, but their scent was different.

A hummingbird whirred to a stop in the air above him, drew a triangle of short flights, then whirred away.

He continued, resting at every switchback. Near the waterfall, he heard a crack and a thump, then turned to see rocks tumbling down the cliff face. Pebble by stone by boulder, the mountains were falling down. He sat and listened to water and wind while clouds gathered. Briefly, a few big drops of rain fell, carried on the wind so that he could see some of them fall almost all the way to the jumbled boulders below, then rise up in the current of air to fly up again, toward him. One drop landed on his forehead like a kiss.

On the way back he walked through the cemetery. He did the usual calculations at the headstones. Eighteen-eighty-seven from 1916. Eighteen-seventy-nine from 1904. Miners had died young. He read the engraving on one particularly showy monument:

ERECTED BY
16 TO 1 MINERS UNION
IN MEMORY OF
JOHN BARTHELL
BORN IN KOVJOKI WORA, FINLAND
DIED AT SMUGGLER, COL.
JULY 3, 1901
AGED 27 YEARS
"In the world's broad field of battle
In the bivouac of life,
Be not like dumb driven cattle
Be a hero in the strife."

Poor bastard, he thought, to die in a mine and then be buried under bad verse. He laughed, enjoying the sound of his own laughter.

By the time he had returned to town, his legs were sore and the sun was going down. He retrieved the Rilke book, then stopped at the Village Market to buy something simple, something a minor poet might eat. Beans. Crackers.

While the beans warmed on the electric stove, he searched the cupboard. There was a set of stylish, mass produced stoneware, but he found what he was looking for in a hand-made bowl with a chipped rim. He held it, feeling in his hands the shape of the hands that had made it.

Eating, he thought about the black damp of the mines. He thought of timbers splintering under the mountain's weight. Bottomless holes that had a bottom after all. Cave-ins. Dust.

He was too old to die young. Far too old. And he didn't think he was going to get in his ten good lines, either. He had always been better at recognizing genius than expressing it.

He washed the dishes in hot water and rinsed them in cold, feeling the difference on his hands. He undressed in one of the bedrooms and then went to stand naked before the bathroom mirror. His body was nothing like the torso of Apollo in Rilke's poem. His pale skin sagged. Veins stood out blue in his wrists and ankles. Looking at this body, another man would have despaired. The man he was yesterday, for example.

II. Metamorphoses

.

Spotted Dolphin

FROM THE EARLIEST DAYS of childhood, the boy dreamed of
buoyancy, of floating through water supported by water, of floating
through the air supported by the air, of floating through space
supported by space. He shared his dreams with his sister. She was a
year older, but willing to follow him. Feathers in their hands, they
jumped from the roof together, learning how to fly.

"You'll get hurt," said their older brother.

They weren't hurt, but they didn't fly, either.

The boy dreamed of galaxies and jellyfish. He liked to lie on his
back in the night grass and listen for the music of the stars.
Sometimes his sister lay on her back beside him. They never heard
anything but the sounds of earthly night: crickets, wind in the trees,
the clatter of kitchen sounds inside the houses. Still, he said he was
sure of the music. Someday he would hear it.

When the older brother grew up, he let life take him up. He
married, fathered children, and worked hard.

When the sister grew up, she let life take her up. She married,
bore children, and was a mother to them.

When the boy grew up, well, there was some doubt that he ever
grew up at all. He went to school for a while. He worked for a

51

while. He had lovers for a while. He was a man now, but he did not become a husband or a father. Mostly, he traveled the world. He told his sister that he still had those dreams of buoyancy, still dreamed of galaxies and jellyfish that were both aglow with the same jeweled light.

He lived for a time in Nepal, in Mexico, in Italy. He had friends in San Francisco and Key West, in Boulder and Madison.

"Why doesn't he make something of himself?" growled the older brother.

"He is," said the sister.

"What?" said the brother. "What is he making of himself?"

But the sister had no words for it.

The man who dreamed of buoyancy learned to meditate. He ate mushrooms that taught him how to cast his soul out of his body like a fishing lure on a silver line. He visited his sister and her family. He made his nephews and nieces laugh with his stories of their mother up on grandma's roof, feathers in her hands, almost flying.

"Don't tell them that!" the sister said.

"You don't want your own children to learn how to fly?"

The man visited his older brother's family, too. The older brother called the sister afterwards. "What's he going to do in his old age? Does he think we'll support him?"

"You would refuse?" said the sister.

"That's not the point."

The man traveled. He lived for a time in Thailand, Australia, Ecuador, and Spain. He stayed with friends in New Orleans, in Taos, and in Boston. He wrote postcards to his sister. He ate pills that taught him how to see farther than the strongest telescopes. He put drops on his tongue that let him hear the songs of dolphins in the ocean deep.

He called her late at night from a city not far from where she lived. He said, "You used to lie in the grass with me, listening to the night sky."

She said, "I remember."

He said, "Help me. I need your help."

"What's wrong?"

"Nothing's wrong," he said. "I can't drive a car with my hands like this."

She came to the place he named. The skin of his hands was gray and spotted. His fingers had grown together. He said, "We have to hurry."

She drove him many miles that night, toward the lowering moon, all the way to the sea. He would not answer her questions, but only recounted their childhood together, the way she had taken up his dreams as if they were her own.

His legs seemed to be joined at the knees. She helped him out of the car and he leaned heavily against her as they crossed the wide beach. Near the water's edge, he fell forward and inched his way along. The dorsal fin ripped his shirt as it grew. His sister felt his desperation for the water, and she pulled him forward by one flipper. Breath puffed out of his blowhole. The sand must be rough against his belly, his sister thought, but then he was far enough for a wave to lift him, and he was free.

Free, his sister thought, looking out over the waves.

His new life had come so suddenly, she had not even said goodbye.

She saw the arch of his fin in the moonlight. She could see his body undulate. He splashed once with his tail and was gone.

His sister stood still for a long time, then mimicked the way he had moved. A wave went from her shoulders, down her spine.

She couldn't follow him. Even so, she stayed there, watching the moon set over the waves, practicing.

The sister called the older brother. She said, "He's gone."

The older brother cried, and he said, "Well, what could we expect after the sort of life he lived?" Later, he told his children that their uncle had died. Much, much later, when the children were almost grown, he cautioned them to choose carefully the lives they would live.

The sister told her children that their uncle had become a dolphin. Much, much later, when the children were almost grown, she told them that by now their uncle might be a celestial body. She led them outside on a summer night. She lay on her back in the damp grass, and her children lay beside her. Together, they listened to the stars.

Rich and Beautiful

In Los Angeles, a man and a woman met.

He said, "How do you like me?"

She said, "You are rich and accomplished." She thought he could be richer and more accomplished if he just worked a little harder, but she didn't say so at first. Then she said, "And how do you like me?"

"You are young and beautiful," he told her. He thought that she could be made even more beautiful with a little surgery, but he kept this to himself.

They married.

"I would love you all the more," she admitted, "if we had not a penthouse, but a mansion."

"And I would love you more than I already do," he confessed, "if your cheekbones were a little higher."

So he worked harder as a deal maker, and she went under the knife. They sold the expensive penthouse and bought a far more expensive mansion. With her new cheekbones, she began a career as a model.

"I'm a lucky man," he said. "Although I'd consider myself luckier if your legs were a bit longer."

"I pretty much completely adore you," she said. "If only we were together in not just a mansion, but an estate with vineyards."

He worked harder than ever, making the deals he had always made and also promoting her as a model. Again, she submitted herself to the surgeons.

With her longer legs she was among the most beautiful women in the world, and her husband and promoter was among the richest men in California. They lived on a wine estate overlooking the sea.

She could imagine him richer. He could imagine her still more beautiful. Each admitted as much.

The surgeons made her lips a little more full, her breasts more round, her waist more narrow. The modeling contracts he negotiated for her brought in higher and higher fees. She was in great demand.

Before long, his most lucrative deals revolved around her beauty. She spent more and more time in surgery, making adjustments. Weeks after each operation, when the swelling had gone down and her scars were undetectable, she would appear in veils to be unwrapped like a treasure for the press. Each time, the world was eager to see how nearly perfect she had become.

For a few days, those who had paid a fortune for the right could pose her and snap her picture. Then, before anyone had much more than glimpsed her, her husband and the surgeons would discuss what was to come next—some alteration of her finger bones, an adjustment to her brow or the width of her mouth.

Now he is richer than Croesus. She is more gorgeous than Aphrodite. Images of her face and hair sell makeup and shampoo. The silhouette of her legs sells cars. A photo of her hand holding a drink sells vacations.

She's invisible much of the time, bandaged or in seclusion. Not even her husband sees her. She is available for only a few sessions a year. Her fees are sky high. Every few months, she emerges for a new unveiling.

He's on the phone day and night, making deals, making plans. His wife is the most appealing woman in the world. Keeping her that way is making him richer and richer.

He hardly sleeps. New opportunities are always appearing.

She hardly exists. Perfection is always a work in progress.

Red-Winged Blackbirds

TO THE THIRD FLOOR OF A glass tower among many glass towers, the men and women came every day to look at gray numbers on the computer screens. They came five days a week, fifty weeks or more a year, to study the numbers and decide whether to buy or sell.

The third floor was close enough to the street that a few trees grew almost to the height of the windows. A man looking out might be hypnotized by the shimmer of sun on dark summer leaves. A woman looking out might feel melancholy for the bare winter branches. But the men and women who worked on the third floor had been chosen for their powers of concentration. Summer or winter, they did not look out of the windows.

It was the custom on the third floor for the men to wear black suits and the women to wear brown dresses. Colors distracted. By design, nothing on the third floor tempted the concentration of the men and women sitting before their screens.

Seasons came and went, as they always do. And always, the men dressed in black and the women dressed in brown attended their work. One winter was particularly long and cold and dark. For weeks on end, the sun did not shine. Rain fell from black clouds and encased the world in ice. The men and women on the third floor worked every day as if they never noticed that the world outside their window was a shadowed tomb.

When at last spring came, the men and women on the third floor paid attention only to their gray numbers even as the first buds outside their windows broke open like green firecrackers. Even as yellow light streamed down from a blue sky, they minded their business. They did not look out through the windows.

Ah, but the heart has eyes of its own. Their hearts saw the yellow light, the green sparks on the trees. Their hearts felt the warmth of spring and stirred inside their chests with the stirring of the spring breeze. But the men and women of the third floor would not be moved. They all kept their attention on their numbers, even though they all felt their hearts strain and beat with feathered wings against the cages of their chests.

A moment before they died, did they know it? Did they touch their hands to their breasts? But if they did, it was too late. Already, their hearts were breaking out, prying open the ribs that caged them. Already, their hearts were bursting into the stale air of the third floor.

Now the men's black feathered hearts filled the air with the flurry of their liberated wings. The brown feathered hearts of the women flew among them.

They were not free. Not yet. They had traded a prison of flesh for a prison of glass. They dashed themselves against the windows, but the glass held.

Was one bird perhaps still more human heart than bird? Was one bird perhaps more passion than feather and bone? For no bird could ever have broken through that window glass. But finally, one did. One bird, or one still-human heart shaped like a bird, hurtled through the pane and fell dead on the other side.

Black birds followed. As each one passed through the broken glass, his shoulders were stained with the blood of the one that had died. Soon the trees outside the window were crowded with birds who sang excitedly for the taste of air and the colors of day. They sang, too, for the hearts of the women to join them.

But the brown birds held back. They circled inside the windows of the third floor, grieving for the lives they had not lived as women.

The black birds in the trees kept calling. By the time the first brown-feathered heart was ready to fly through the broken window, the blood had dried on the glass and did not mark her wings. She flew to a branch. One by one, the others followed her.

Now the red-winged blackbirds arrive with the first breath of spring. The males are first and must sing day after day to coax the females to forget the lives they once knew. "Come," sing the hearts of the men. "Come and live in the spring that is now unfolding. The sky is blue. The world burns with green fire. Come!"

Alephestra

The gods used to decorate the night sky with mortals they would honor or punish, save or condemn. Cassiopeia sits upon a heavenly throne, immortalized for her beauty. Yet for her vanity, the sky revolves and turns her on her head. Castor and Pollux must dwell at times in the underworld, but Jupiter so admired their brotherly love that on some nights they look down from the sky where all is perfection. The young hunter, Arcas, circles the pole star and is forever about to slay the bear that he thinks is charging him. He did not know, and will never know, that the beast rushes not to attack, but to embrace him. She is his mother, Callisto, altered by a jealous curse. To prevent the shame and horror of Callisto's murder, Jupiter hurled son and mother into the heavens where the fatal thrust will never come, but where we must see poor Arcas every night and be reminded of the thing he is always about to do.

So it is with other constellations, stars, and heavenly lights. Mortals beyond counting or remembering have gone from this sphere to that higher one.

One time, though, the transformation was in the other direction. Long ago, the world had not the one moon we see now, but two. The second, smaller moon was called Alephestra, though some say that she wasn't truly the second moon, but the first. She was a

63

goddess, but one of modest station and powers, or else she was a titan, or some being even more ancient. She never visited the earth. Instead she looked upon the blue world from the distance and praised it. The clouds were beautiful to her. Oceans gleamed in the sun. Although she had seen neither leaf nor grove, she would praise trees for their beauty. Although she had never seen mortal man or woman, she loved the stories that gods told about them.

For a long time, the little moon's talk amused Jupiter. He would ask her to describe the deer, the flowers, and the new-plowed fields of earth. She told him about the rainbow colors of fish scales even though she had never seen rainbows or fish, and he smiled with what may have been indulgence. When she compared the smell of a wet bear to the odor of a man wearing a woolen cloak and told Jove that a bear on its hind legs in the rain was very hard to tell apart from a man, he nodded and smiled a different sort of smile. When she said that flower nectar was like the nectar of Olympus, he laughed. Alephestra knew that his pleasure was sometimes at her expense, but she had no way to know which of her impressions were correct and which were mistaken. Besides, whatever details she might have misunderstood, she remained certain that the earth was more wondrous than the heavens. And one way or another, her descriptions and pronouncements always pleased Jupiter.

One day, however, the old lightning hurler was in a bad mood. Some mortal maiden had refused his advances, and he sat among the stars, glowering at earth. When Alephestra glided near, she saw the way his face was twisted. Jupiter in a bad mood was dangerous, and anyone who could would have avoided him. But Alephestra's orbit was fixed. She could neither alter her path nor hurry past him. Instead of drifting by in silence, she tried to please him. She began to sing about the sacred groves and the honor that mortals paid to trees.

Jupiter commanded her to be silent. The world of mortals was nothing like what she imagined. Mortals might esteem a sacred grove here or there, but they despoiled whole forests to make pasture for their sheep or for firewood. Whatever beauty there was on the earth was fleeting. Grasp mortal loveliness as you might here or there, it would elude you somewhere else. And all that was beautiful on earth fell at last to rot and ruin. The world below was not worthy of song.

Perhaps Alephestra could not hear him as she sang. She kept singing.

Jupiter is not a god of second chances. Annoyed, he sent Alephestra hurtling toward the earth. As she fell, she took the shape of a woman. If she could not stop singing the praises of the imperfect world, let her see it for herself.

Like a fallen star, the moon struck the sea with a thunderclap and the hiss of steam. All around her was blackness as she settled to the bottom of the abyss. Truly, earth was not as she had been told, and still less than she had imagined. There was nothing at all to see.

Even so, the taste of salt was novel to her, and the cold embrace of water against her skin was nothing like celestial ether. Disappointed though she was, she was fascinated, too. On the bottom of the sea, she discovered the sensation of walking. In time, she wandered high enough to encounter light, and finally air. She walked ashore in a place where mountains met the sea. For the first time, Alephestra saw trees. She heard the waves breaking at her feet and the cries of gulls. She stood amazed. Apollo's chariot slowly crossed the sky, and the shifting shadows amazed Alephestra. The colors of the sunset made her sigh. Stars burned forth. Tides rose and fell around her, and she did not move from where she stood.

She might have stayed rooted to the spot if Jupiter had not happened to notice her. The father god had recovered from his disappointment as soon as another maiden had caught his fancy. But he remembered his annoyance when he saw how delighted Alephestra was with the world. He dispatched Mercury to show her the worst that the earthly realm had to offer.

Mercury saw how Alephestra admired a virgin forest, so he took her to the hills around a city where men were cutting the last trees. Alephestra knelt beside a broken stump in awe of the fresh wood's color and smell. The messenger showed her war. She was fascinated by the scarlet wounds and the smell of flesh. He opened graves for her, and she sighed with pleasure to see corruption and the feast of worms. The world of mortals was not at all what she had expected, but everything about it amazed her. Mercury showed her everything that was base. Nothing displeased her. When he had run out of ideas, Mercury returned to tell the father god of the little moon's ceaseless fascination. On her own Alephestra continued to walk the world, astonished by the shimmer of moonlight on a river, the sound of wind blowing over dunes, the smell of smoke, of mildew, of blossoms. She sampled the taste of dew, of copper, of ashes. She kept moving. When Mercury returned with orders to restore her to her place in the sky, he could not find her.

She never was returned to her place in the heavens. She moved from one delight to another, never lingering. Astonished, then gone.

When we gaze into the red depths of a canyon or across an expanse of rusting steel, she sees the same blade of tender grass that we see. She may be watching the smoke curl from a cigarette or listening as a key rasps in the lock. Where white blossoms open or a poisoned animal lies down to die, her sighs mingle with the breeze. She is always here. She is always already gone.

Periwinkles

"HERE'S A PARABLE."

"Tell me a riddle instead. Your parables never make sense."

"They do if you listen carefully not just to what I say but to what I don't say."

"That's a poor excuse. What is this parable about?"

"Good and evil."

"All right, I'll listen."

"Once there was a man who was good. And when he died —"

"Wait a minute! What do you mean by good? Was he pious?"

"I'm not sure."

"Then how was he good? What was his moral foundation?"

"His goodness might have had a philosophical basis rather than a religious one."

"What did he do that was good?"

"He was generous. Where he saw people in need, he gave what he could afford."

"Ha! I know people who give nothing at all because they believe they can't afford it."

"Well, he also forgave injuries when it was reasonable to forgive them."

"So turn the other cheek, but only when it's reasonable."

"If a stranger is stabbing your child, do you say at once, 'I forgive you'? Do you offer up your other child?"

"Of course not!"

"Goodness isn't simple. But he *was* good. When he died, he happened to die alone in a forest."

"Wait. If he was good, why didn't he die in the company of those who loved him?"

"It didn't happen that way. He died alone beneath a tree, and his body lay undiscovered."

"They would have looked for him."

"They didn't find him. Fallen leaves hid his remains. Moth and maggot transformed his clothes into soil. Mice gnawed at his skeleton. In time, periwinkles sprouted. From the earth that had once been this good man there arose a hundred blue flowers."

"A traveler would come across that place and feel at peace."

"Perhaps. Now at about the same time there was a man who was evil, and when he died —"

"Evil how?"

"The opposite of the first."

"Greedy."

"Yes."

"But *evil*. I suppose he might have been a rapist."

"Whose parable is this?"

"I want specifics."

"He was evil. And he happened to die alone in a forest."

"The same forest?"

"Yes."

"How did he die? Was he stoned to death?"

"Alone, I said."

"He should have been executed."

"It didn't happen that way. He died alone and his body lay undiscovered."

"You can bet that no one went looking for *him*."

"The worst tyrants have their admirers. In any case, no one found him. In time the earth reclaimed him. Periwinkles sprouted."

"Not periwinkles. It should be thistles."

"It wasn't. It was periwinkles again."

"This place wouldn't feel the same though. A traveler would come across this carpet of flowers and feel foreboding."

"He might. Or he might feel at peace."

"But it shouldn't be the same flowers, the same mood in both places!"

"Can you stand over a grave and know the character of the stranger whose name is on the stone?"

"Of course not. But this is a parable! It's supposed to illustrate something."

"It does."

Sea Anemones

IN A LITTLE CHURCH BY the sea, long after the old gods had begun to sleep, there was a preacher of the Christian gospel who earnestly worried for the souls of his congregants. He wanted every one of them to one day arrive safe in the Father God's heaven, so he harangued and exhorted them about all the temptations that might lead them astray. He was particularly worried about the sorts of love and lust that Father God had condemned.

He had a strong voice and chose his words well. His predecessor, though no less earnest, had been a stoop-shouldered, colorless little man. For listeners in the last pews, this previous preacher's drone from the pulpit was sometimes lost in the sound of waves crashing against the rocky shore. Old people dozed. So did some who were not so old.

This current preacher, though, belted out his verses and his warnings loud enough to wake *any* sleeper. "Men," he cried, "can you *imagine* lying with another man, receiving him as you would have your wives receive you? Women, can you *imagine* kissing and embracing another woman as you would your husband?" There were other kinds of love prohibited by the Father God, but the preacher often dwelt on these particular sins, his voice thick with a disgust that his listeners could not help but feel themselves. No,

71

they could not, dared not imagine the sort of passion that the Father God had prohibited. "Unnatural acts. Ungodly, and unnatural acts!"

These words, carried on a thunderous voice, vibrated in the ear of Cupid, who woke from that slumber that the old gods had been sleeping these many centuries. The son of Venus felt provoked by what he heard.

As Apollo learned long ago, it is dangerous to provoke Cupid. The sun god, boasting about the sky python he had killed with an arrow, said that it was the shoulder that made the archer. He compared his massive arms to Cupid's and concluded that while Cupid might carry a bow, it was but a toy compared to the charioteer's. Cupid replied that a hunter is known by his prey, and that if he felled Apollo, didn't that make him the greater archer? He sent a golden arrow into Apollo's heart and a leaden one into the daughter of Peneus. Apollo could think of nothing else but this girl who suddenly despised all thoughts of men or marriage, and he never did win her.

Not only slander, but subtler things might provoke Cupid. He felt irked by his mother's constant demands. "Shoot Neptune, my son! Let's rouse the cool sea god to feverish passion. Oh, there's Ceres, trying to keep her tasty daughter a virgin forever. Put an arrow into Pluto, my boy, and show that even Mister Gloom can't resist us." She picked mortal targets for him, too, as if she forgot whose arrows these were. So one day when she embraced him fondly, as a mother will do, he let a golden arrow graze her breast. A mere scratch, he gave her. She did not even notice the injury, but she did notice the mortal Adonis, a hunter. They made an unlikely pair, for Venus thought that traipsing through the woods and stabbing animals was the sort of work best left to servants or cold-hearted Diana, who never cared how she looked before men, anyway, with her troupe of girls who admired the huntress for her skill and wit more than her beauty. But Venus! Hunting! She would never have imagined herself doing anything of the sort.

That was a sight, then, the goddess of love in her filmy gowns getting twigs in her hair and dirt on her sandaled feet, following Adonis from one bloody scene to another.

So Cupid went to this church by the sea, offended. He would shoot where he pleased, and how dare any mortal express such disgust at some of the results? He sat in the rafters, rubbing centuries of sleep from his eyes, and listened. When the preacher said again, "Just imagine...," Cupid smiled.

His arrows never were his only weapon, merely the most selective. Cupid's quiver also held stoppered bottles, and one of these he uncorked to pour a golden mist over the congregation. For the first time, in all the times the preacher had said, "Just imagine," they could. "Just imagine, men, accepting another man as your lover." And the men imagined their hearts full of longing for another man. "Women, just imagine that you would have another woman standing in the place where God has given you your husbands." And the women imagined their lips burning for another woman's kiss.

As the mist was not selective, neither was its effect. The men felt the lure of no particular man; the women lusted for no particular woman. The embraces they imagined were general, universal, and joyous. Even the preacher felt the effect of the mist, though it reached him last. He paused, thinking a pleasant thought about his hand closing tenderly around...

But, no, he would fight this thought. This was wrong, and he would summon the will to be disgusted, though there was a fire in his blood now. The congregation sat stiff, in more ways than one, not daring to move, willing themselves to stop thinking what they could not cease to think.

These were pious people. They had been schooled all their lives to revile the sin of indiscriminate love. Their mortal souls were at stake.

Cupid didn't care. He poured it on, unstopping another vial of his funky mist, and then another. What the congregation began to feel was beyond sin, as everything in that spare sanctuary seemed to undulate and wink and promise. The wood grain of the pulpit swirled and twined with breathtaking beauty. The virginal white walls seemed made for caressing. The hard pews pressed so lovingly against back and buttocks that one woman groaned aloud with pleasure.

With that groan went the last of their resistance, except for one tiny gasp from the preacher and his one word, "No." Then they were all gazing in rapture at the room around them, at each other. They tasted the perfume of ordinary air, wanted to embrace the earth itself. They felt the tender caresses of their clothes for the first time, the erotic whisper of cloth against their skin.

They might have fallen upon one another, men on women on women on men on men, but the desire they felt was not merely for each other, but for everything. A breath coming in was a lover arriving. A breath going out was a lover's momentary, aching departure.

They spilled out of the church, wanting the rough or smooth bark of the trees, the bright lovesong of birds, the sensations of grass and sky and sand. They wanted everything all at once, and could not choose among their many lovers until someone, it may even have been the preacher himself, said, "The sea!"

The sea was a lover that would embrace each body everywhere at once. The sea was a lover vast enough to receive them. They ran, hearts pounding with lust and joy. Across the tide pools they ran, scattering seagulls that they loved, glimpsing starfish that they loved, thinking tenderly of the limpet's embrace of the thoroughly embraceable rocks, but not pausing for any of these. They ran, feet splashing into the sea.

Some fell and cut their hands and knees on the jagged barnacles that they loved. They got up. They kept going, wading out to let the sea embrace their knees, to soak through their clothes to their loins, to accept them up to their chests, their shoulders, their ears. They tasted the salt of this lover who could be, for a moment at least, all lovers. Their mouths filled with the sea's kisses.

Cupid would have let them drown.

Their splashing and tasting, the thrusting of their hips in the water, their answering undulations to the waves...all of this roused Neptune. Is it any wonder? Who would not be roused from sleep by that?

The sea god looked into their hearts and saw what they wanted. He touched them with his weedy fingers, and their feet held firm to the sea floor. They shrank beneath the waves, softening, yielding, their mouths puckering for a kiss. With another touch, Neptune removed from them any memory of what they had been before, male or female, and made each a bit of both.

They are there to this day, clinging to the bottom of the sea, loving the water, loving the rocks beneath them, loving the fish that they hug with their tentacles in an embrace that ends with digestion, for they kept the aching effects of Cupid's spell. No one but the archer himself can undo that.

Desire is always with them. It overcomes them on nights of the full moon when the water grows cloudy with their sperm and starry with their eggs.

Gold

"HERE'S A ANOTHER PARABLE."

"Wait. Before you go on, I want you to say what this story is going to be about."

"You should listen first and then decide."

"Are you afraid of speaking plainly?"

"I tell these stories as plainly as you will allow. Now, there was a man who was always in pain."

"Why? What ailed him?"

"He had a crooked back, let's say."

"Was he born that way?"

"Possibly. I think so. Yes."

"It sounds as if you're making this up as you go along."

"I make stories as I make my life."

"So life is like a story. That's what you're saying."

"No. What I'm saying is that there was a man who was always in pain. And he endured. No man, woman, or child ever heard him complain."

"Does that mean he never complained?"

"It means what I said."

"So who does that leave? He might have muttered when no one could hear him. He might have complained to God. What was the man's religion?"

"That's not part of the story."

"It would be if I were telling it. And if this man never complained, how did anyone know that he was in pain?"

"I didn't say yet that anyone knew of it. But they did. They could see it in his eyes. Sometimes in his sleep, he groaned."

"Ha! That's a sort of complaint!"

"In his sleep, I said. The thing that pained him most in his waking hours was labor."

"What kind of work?"

"He was a wood cutter."

"Not very suitable work for a man with a crooked back if you ask me."

"It was the path open to him. He provided for his wife, his son, and his daughter."

"If he had complained some, they might have been more help to him."

"It was a hard enough life for all of them. They already helped as they could."

"But he was in pain. He should have said so."

"Suppose someone gives you a gift and then complains of what it cost."

"I see. That's the clearest you have ever been. Thank you."

"Now when the man died, the family dug a grave for him and tried to carry him to it. He was too heavy."

"You should have said at the beginning that he was a big man."

"He wasn't. He had grown very heavy in death. The son gathered distant neighbors, and six men staggered beneath the weight of the corpse. Before they reached the graveside, they dropped him. His back broke open like a purse, and out spilled what might have been nuggets of gold."

"Gold. How would people so poor know gold when they saw it?"

"It might have been gold. It shone. It was heavy."

"So they were rich?"

"The son insisted that the gold, if gold it was, must be buried with his father. And this was done."

"If these people were so poor, they wouldn't act that way around gold. Didn't someone pocket a nugget or two?"

"The family was grieving. The neighbors didn't dare."

"This was their big chance! They sound like idiots."

"Later, some thieves heard the story and tried to rob the grave. They found no gold, nor even bones."

"So they were digging in the wrong spot."

"The family went on as before. The son took his father's place. In their modest way, they prospered."

"Aha! So they had dug up the gold!"

"I mean only that the daughter married, that the son found a wife and cared for his mother in her old age. They were never anything but poor."

"Maybe it wasn't gold, then."

"Perhaps not."

Rag Monster

LET'S NOT BOTHER WITH THE details of how she started saving scraps of cloth. It might have been that she was poor and such scraps were the only thing at the orphanage that she could call her own. It might have been that she was wealthy and began saving scraps of cloth when, as a student at an elite private college, she had stained a favorite dress with Cabernet and had cut out squares of material before she threw the rest away. It doesn't matter exactly who she was or how she began.

What does matter is this: She loved quilts. She intended to make one.

She kept the fabric scraps in a closet. She added to the collection, scrounging and scrimping, perhaps, or perhaps buying whatever caught her eye.

She added more material. She considered how this color or pattern went with that one. She looked at finished quilts in the homes of her friends or on the walls of museums. More and more of her thoughts were devoted to the quilts that she would make.

Always, just as she was about to start to pin one of her designs together, something came up. She had a romance, or a baby, or a divorce, or another baby, or a job, or a promotion, or a death in the family, or a drinking problem, or an auto accident, or a suicidal

81

depression. Every time she was about to begin her first quilt, life intruded. Or if life didn't intrude, she would put her hand on the closet door and suddenly feel very tired, too tired to begin anything so involved as a quilt.

In the midst of this, she grew old. In the midst of growing old, she died.

On the day that she died, the closet door opened. The heap of fabric fell into the hallway. The front door opened. The scraps got outside.

How? They might have crept or oozed or shuffled. No one saw the pile move. No one ever sees it move. But it does move. It appears in one place and then in another.

One day, the mound of rags is on the sidewalk outside of the Greyhound station. A man who has just gotten off the bus sees the heap, considers, then goes back inside the station to buy a ticket for the next city north.

Later, a mother watching her baby play in the park thinks she sees something in the bushes. She gets a closer look. It's just a heap of dirty, tattered rags. Even so, she scoops her child up and hurries away.

In the desert, an artist paints a landscape that has the rag monster in it. The monster is dark, indistinct, and could almost be another boulder. But it isn't. The painting doesn't sell. Even after the artist paints over the pile of rags to place a boulder there—definitely a boulder—people look at the painting and can sense that somewhere in it, something is terribly wrong.

Ghost Fever

Alternative Names: Juruá River fever; Yanani fever; river palsy; eros agitans; kissing flu.

Definition: A disorder characterized by fever, shaking, inappetence, and myalgia.

Symptoms, causes, and incidence: Ghost fever presents with the sudden onset of high fever and headache, followed somewhat later by muscle and joint pains and tremors. These major symptoms then subside but recur in cycles of 48 to 72 hours. In the interim, affected people experience difficulty concentrating and loss of appetite.

The cause of ghost fever is not known, though the symptoms are suggestive of both Dengue fever and Malaria. No infectious agent, viral or parasitic, has been identified, but the pattern of infection suggests that the disease is transmitted by the bite of mosquitos.

The disease is endemic to the Juruá River in western Brazil and is seen in many travelers who visit the area. The disease is self-limiting and most symptoms generally do not persist for long after a visitor has departed the region, except for a dull ache in the bones which patients may continue to complain of for an indefinite period.

The disease is never seen far from the Juruá and its tributaries.

Folk etiology: The following is transcribed from an interview with a native *curandeira*:

"Yanani was just a girl. No one remembers just what she looked like. Were her eyes green or brown? Was the curve of her limbs delicate or voluptuous? She was beautiful, certainly. And she had a way of moving that drew the eye.

"The old women in her village watched her, and they watched how the men watched her. There was bound to be trouble. She was the kind of girl who knew she was being watched, and liked it. She practiced how she walked. She refined the orbit of her hips. A girl like that can be a fire leaping from house to house, even if she does nothing more than enjoy how the men are looking at her.

"And it wasn't just the men. When Yanani went to the river to wash her family's clothes, she brushed by the wives and sisters, touching them casually in a way that hinted of caresses sweeter than any man's. She perfected a glance just for women. When she cupped her hands to hold water, no woman could fail to imagine being held that way. Even the old women felt it. There was bound to be trouble, indeed.

"Everyone wanted her, even boys too young for such longings, even the men who had never wanted any woman. Word of her was whispered from village to village. Men and sometimes women came from as far away as the waterfalls to glimpse her.

"One of the old women decided to head off the trouble. She took Yanani aside and told her, "Oh, granddaughter, you know how you make this man's pulse leap or that woman's hands tremble. You know how you make everyone burn. But you are mortal, girl. Some day a man will plant a little seed in your womb. You will have babies. You will grow matronly and fat. In time, you will look just like me with all my wrinkles. Think about that."

"Yanani did think about the woman's words, but what she

thought was that she wanted to prove the old woman wrong. She wanted this power to stay with her forever.

"One night, Yanani rose while the village slept. She went to the river bank and prayed to the moon god, that worker of night miracles.

"The moon hears many prayers. He does not answer many. But Yanani did more than pray. She wove a dance, an offering, out of every gesture that had stopped men's breaths or made women touch their mouths with their fingers. And the moon came down. She gave herself to him, and he filled her body with his light.

"'What do you want?' the moon asked.

She told him.

"'Be careful,' he cautioned, but she said again that she did not want her powers ever to diminish. So he granted her wish. He held her in the white light of his arms, and she melted away. All that was left of her was her sigh, and its power.

"She rides the breezes, now and always. Come to the river, and she will find you. It does not matter if you are too young, too old, too uninterested in virginal girls. She will mix her breath with yours, will sink into your bones, and you will want her. You will tremble and sweat with longing. The fever will come. You won't be able to eat. She will be the whole world to you, even though all you know of her is your desire."

Prevention: Because the disease may be spread by mosquito bite, personal protection (mosquito netting, repellent, adequate clothing, etc.) may offer a degree of prophylaxis. However, until the cause of the disease is more clearly understood, the only sure method of prevention is to avoid travel to the Juruá River and vicinity.

Treatment: Rehydration, if dehydration is evident. Acetaminophen Or aspirin for aches and fever.

Folk treatment: The following is transcribed from an interview with a native *curandeira*:

"How would you put an end to passion? What is the cure for lust? She is not here to receive you, so you will not quench your fire that way. Alcohol may make you feel better, or worse. Another lover may transform your aching, or only make you all the more feverish for what you cannot have. Sometimes there is nothing to do but suffer. With time, it won't be so bad. But she'll always be with you, deep in your bones. You will always ache for her a little, even when you are old like me."

Prognosis: Full recovery is expected, though an ill-defined ache may persist indefinitely.

Don Ysidro

ON THAT LAST MORNING, anyone who came to visit me could see that I was dying. I knew it myself. As if I had cotton in my ears, I heard the voice of don Leandro saying to my wife, "Doña Susana, I think it is time to fetch the priest," and I thought, yes, it's time. We don't have our own priest, or even our own church, so someone has to drive in a pickup truck to get the priest from El Puentecito. But don't be fooled by what you may hear in Malpasa or in Palpan de Baranda. Here we remain Catholic. Yes, we make pots in the old way. That's why tourists come here. And it's true, as is sometimes whispered, that we have restored certain other practices from the past. But not as they were done back then. Those were bloody and terrible times, the times of the Mejica. They say that the sacrificial blood covered the sun pyramids from top to bottom. Thank the Virgin, we don't do anything like that.

A little after the priest came and went, I died. Word spread. People came to our house. My family asked first for things of mine that they wanted. Then the other neighbors. Don Francisco stood near my body and said, "Don Ysidro, may I have your shovel? I need one, and your sons-in-law can dig new clay for Susana."

I said, "Take it with my blessing."

Susana said, "He says for you to take it."

Next was doña Eustacia. She asked for one of my *seguetas* for scraping pots.

I said, "Of course. Go with my blessing," and Susana said, "He says for you to take it."

When don Tomás came, he asked for my boots, the ones of red leather with the roosters in the stitching.

I said, "Tomás, you thieving rascal! I know very well that you took two of my chickens that night seven years ago to feed to your whore from Puebla. And here you come asking not for a *segueta* or some wire, but for my good boots!"

And Susana said, "He says for you to take them." Because, of course, she couldn't hear me. In any case, I would have let Tomás have the boots. I only wanted to see him blush just one time.

They came and asked for everything that Susana would not need. They asked even for things for which it was not necessary to ask. They asked for things I had already promised to them. They even asked for permission to dig white clay from the place where I liked to find it. They asked, and I said yes, with my blessings. We are nothing if not polite.

Last of all, they asked for a few of my hairs to make brushes for painting pots. They cut what locks there were with scissors. They asked for my hands and cut them off with a knife for butchering goats. They said, "Don Ysidro, we want your face." I agreed, and they flayed off the skin very carefully and tenderly. They put my hands in a metal drum and burned them. They dried my face in the sun. Meanwhile, they wrapped the rest of my body in a shroud and buried it in the churchyard according to the customs of the Church.

For a time after that, I was in an emptiness, a nowhere place. I didn't see. I didn't hear. I couldn't speak. I wasn't anywhere, not in my house, not in the coffin in the ground. Nowhere. But that would change.

All my life, I had taught the other people of my village to make pots as I made them. That was nothing special. We all did this. I made my own don Ysidro pots, except when doña Isabela showed me how to make her little tiny ones, or don Marcos demonstrated how he painted his. Then for a while, I would make little tiny pots just like doña Isabela or pots painted in the style of don Marcos. When doña Jenífera had gone to the capital to see the birds and animals on ancient pots, she imitated those decorations, showed us, and soon we all knew how to do it. The rest of the time, I made pots in my own manner, though sometimes with a little touch of Isabela or Marcos or Jenífera that I had learned from them and made my own.

Now for the week after I had died, everyone in the village would be making pots as I had made them. Even the children, if they were old enough to make pots of their own. They dug white clay from my favorite place, soaked it, filtered it, let it settle, and poured off the clear water from the slurry. When the clay was dry enough, they mixed in the ashes of my hands. Then they made clay tortillas and pressed them into big plaster molds for the base, just like the ones I used. Sometimes they used my very own molds. They made snakes of clay, attached them to the bases, wound them around from the bottom up. My pots didn't have necks. Neither did these. The people—my family and all the rest of the town—scraped these pots smooth, rubbed them to a shine, and painted them with black paint, using brushes of my own hair and in designs I would have used: lizards and rabbits with checkered backs, or else just checkers that started big around the middle of the pot and became intricate at the lip. Those were pots in the don Ysidro style. They fired them. The ones that the fire didn't break, they brought to my house. Susana put pots all around the front room, and even in the bed where I had lain.

But I didn't see this. I only knew it was happening.

These pots in my house sat undisturbed. The people burned the brushes made from my hair.

On the third day, there was a feast at my house. Probably there were all kinds of tamales, some with olives and meat, some with seeds and beans. Men and women drank pulque, and there was perhaps melon water for the children. The sun went down. Candles were lit. A fire burned in my fireplace.

At midnight, don Leandro opened a box and took out the mask made of my own skin. He put my face over his face, and I opened our eyes. I came from the place that was nowhere. I was in the room. I looked at the faces, at the wide eyes of the living, at Susana holding her hand over her mouth. I saw my grandchildren, Carlos and Jalea, Ana and Quinito. And for the first time, I could see the pots in the living room. They glowed in the candlelight. Together, don Leandro and I went into the bedroom and I saw the pots there on the bed. We returned to the living room, and I said with our mouth, "I see that I am not dead after all!"

"No, no, don Ysidro," they assured me. "You are not dead!"

I laughed. That's what you feel like doing when you see that you aren't dead.

Then don Leandro threw the mask into the fire, and I wasn't in the mask any more. I was in the pots. In all those round pots made by the hands of my friends, my rivals, my family, my neighbors. I was there, in each one. The people took me away from my house, pot by pot, and I entered their houses with them. In my former home, they left only the pot that Susana had made in my style.

From that night forward, I was all over the village. People stored corn in me, or rice, or beans. They used me to carry water. And I spread out from there, for if tourists came to buy pots and happened to admire me, the potter would say, "Oh, that's don Ysidro." And the tourist would nod and perhaps buy the pot that he thought was merely *made* by don Ysidro.

I am still in my little village, but I am in Stockholm, too, and Seattle. I am in Toronto and Buenos Aires. Some of me is in Mexico, the capital, though I am mostly still at home here in the village where I grew up, grew old, and died. I sit on Susana's shelf where I can watch her make ordinary tortillas for her breakfast or clay tortillas for her pots. She is old, but her hands are still quick as birds. Sometimes she knows that I am watching her, and she looks over her shoulder and laughs. Whether she can hear it or not, my answering laughter is deep and full and round like a great big pot in the manner of don Ysidro.

III. Insurrections

Murder, Mystery

OKAY, THIS IS A MURDER MYSTERY. The victim is lying in a field not far from U.S. 36. Face down.

It's early morning. Along the eastern horizon there's a band of clouds, though the sky overhead is blue. The sun is up, but still hidden. Here's what I want you to see: to the west, another cloud bank lies against the Flatirons, with just the jagged tops of the first and third Flatirons jutting through. I've already said the sky is blue, but I don't think you've really seen it. Brilliant blue? Piercing blue? At this distance, you can see the summits of Longs Peak and Mount Meeker, capped with snow and orange in the early light.

See it? See the bright orange mountains against the blue sky? See the clouds hugging the Flatirons? Can you sense what the light is like for someone standing in this field? (There is no one standing there, of course. There's just the body, and the body is lying down.) A western meadowlark sings. They only sing at certain levels of light, early in the day and early in the evening. The song is like this: three bright, slow notes, then a flurry of song too fast and complex to describe. You can hold the sound in your mind for only a moment, then the memory of it melts away.

I know what you're thinking.

We'll get to the body, I promise. But first I want to be certain you can see the light, the two banks of clouds, the orange mountains, the blue sky behind them. It's spring. The foothills are green. Soon the sun will rise a little more and burn those clouds from the Flatirons. You'll see just how green the hills are. The western meadowlark will stop singing.

There's heavy traffic on U.S. 36, but no one has seen the body. Cars swish by. Anyone could spot this body. It's right here in the field.

It looks as if the dead man was shot in the back and fell forward. There's not much blood around the hole in the back of his shirt. The exit wound is probably another story.

Was he killed here? Did he expect it? Were there two men holding his arms while another pointed the gun? What caliber of gun was it? Was he a drug dealer? Witness to another crime? Jealous husband? The lover? Maybe the wife killed him. Maybe he didn't expect it. Maybe he was killed somewhere else and brought here, dumped here.

The soil in the field is soft. There are footprints. Someone will be able to tell the story, or part of it, anyway, by looking at those footprints. They'll figure out the caliber of the gun. They'll identify the man and unravel his history, interview suspects.

But we won't.

This is not that kind of a mystery.

His face is against the ground, but turned a little.

At this time of year, at this time of morning, there's something about the smell of earth and growing grass.

The man's lips are parted. His tongue juts a little between his teeth. It's as if he's tasting the dew on the grass.

That's not a symbol or anything. That's just the way it is.

I wish I had a word for the blue of the sky.

Vocabulary Items

Choose the appropriate word to complete the following sentences.

1. As citizens we would be _____ if we did not make these facts public.

A. derelict
B. dirigible
C. discreet
D. detritus

In the city council chamber, the floor was opened for public comment. Two citizens came to the microphone.

Ms. Patricia Wilson, who was represented by Mr. Kyle in the Sixth Ward said: "My friend Amy, who is a nurse at the VA hospital, she can get me as much Percodan as I want. And I want a lot."

Mr. Jim Smitts, who was represented by Ms. Turnbull in the First Ward said: "I'd just like to say one thing? My neighbor across the street, he's got a daughter? She's fourteen? And she's real cute? And I seen her washing her Daddy's car, and she was wearing shorts and she got wet? And now I'm sitting in my living room all the time, looking over there and hoping to see something like that again? That's all I'd like to say."

The correct answer is C.

2. Many administrative assistants fail because they are not sufficiently _____.

A. versatile
B. voracious
C. varicolored
D. venal

On his way to a board meeting, Mr. Matthews stopped by Jane's desk. "Pull the files on the Brandywine account for me," he said. "I'd like to review them when I get back this afternoon."

"They'll be on your desk."

"Is that letter ready for my signature?"

She gave him the letter. He signed it.

"Oh," he said, "and I noticed on my way in that there's a Cape buffalo by the water cooler."

"Is there?" said Jane.

"Yes. A dead one. Take care of it, will you?"

"Of course." She got up from her desk to have a look.

The buffalo was a big one, weighing many hundreds of pounds. It lay on its side, eyes open. Jane put her hand on one massive hoof and pushed. The leg yielded. The buffalo hadn't been dead for long.

Jane knew that an animal of this size was more than she could handle alone, so she went from office to office, from cubicle to cubicle, gathering the other administrative assistants. Then Jane crouched close to the buffalo. With her powerful claws, she tore open the still-warm carcass and used her teeth to rip out a gobbet of flesh. The other administrative assistants fell to, as well. Soon their hands and faces were smeared with blood. They gorged on flesh until they could eat no more. Then they retreated to their work stations to doze a while and renew their appetites.

However, even after a second round of feeding, the buffalo was scarcely half devoured when Mr. Matthews returned from his meeting. He scowled at Jane. "Is that all?" he said. "You've barely started on the entrails, and one of the forelegs hasn't even been touched!" He shook his head. "I'm sorry to say this, Jane, but I'm going to have to let you go." He looked at the others. "You, too. The lot of you. You're all *fired*!"

The correct answer is B.

3. The best way to choose a soldier for a suicide mission is to pick someone _____ by drawing lots.

A. rationally
B. randomly
C. repeatedly
D. retroactively

The night before the selection was to be made, the officers gathered in the Colonel's bunker to decide which of the enlisted men they most disliked. It came down to Mimsby, Hawkins and Pimm. The officers then considered which of these three men, by his permanent absence from the trenches, might actually have a positive impact on morale. Without a doubt, the answer was Pimm, but he was so defective that he might not be able to carry off even a simple suicide mission. Hawkins seemed the next best choice until one of the captains said he rather *liked* Hawkins playing the harmonica of an evening, and maybe not *all* the enlisted chaps hated it. Perhaps those who enjoyed the harmonica simply hadn't spoken up. So the officers settled on Mimsby. In the morning, one of the majors went among the men with a bundle of sticks. Short stick would draw the mission. "Don't pick the blue one," the major said to each man in turn, and when he came at last to Mimsby, there was only one stick left, the one painted blue. It was the short stick.

"Sorry about that, lad," major told him. "Luck of the draw, what?"

The correct answer is A.

4. Mr. Evans objected to the day care center next to his home because the children were _____.

A. obstreperous
B. ovoid
C. officious
D. obsequious

"Good Lord, but they are noisy today," Mrs. Evans said.

Mr. Evans grunted, put down his paper, and went to the open window. "Hey!" he shouted. "Pipe down out there!"

"Sorry, Mr. Evans," said one of the children.

"We didn't mean to disturb you," said another.

"We appreciate your letting us know that we were getting out of hand," said a third. "We're happy to have you as neighbors. We appreciate some contact with the older, wiser generation."

"We'll try to play more quietly now. Don't hesitate to tell us if we're bothering you again."

"Yeah, okay," said Mr. Evans, and to his wife he said, "God, they give me the creeps!"

She said, "I know what you mean."

A few minutes later, the doorbell rang. It was the children. "My, you are looking well today, Mrs. Evans," said one of the boys. "Have you lost weight?"

"Why, no, I... What can I do for you?"

"Is Mr. Evans home?"

Mr. Evans came to the door. "What?"

"Mr. Evans, we couldn't help noticing that the leaves are collecting in your gutters. You really ought to do something about that."

"I don't see how that's any business of yours," said Mr. Evans. "Go away."

"Mr. Evans, those leaves could eventually block your down spouts," said a girl. "You could get water under your eaves, and dry rot."

Another girl added, "You can buy a plastic gutter scoop at Home Depot for under five dollars, a very good price, I'm sure you'll agree."

"Or," said a boy, "you could let us clean out your gutters. We'd be happy to do it at no cost to you. Just say the word!"

"No," said Mr. Evans. He closed the door and shivered.

"I know," said Mrs. Evans. "They are so unnaturally helpful and polite for children."

"Polite, hell!" said Mr. Evans. "Haven't you noticed the shape of their *heads*?"

The correct answer is B.

Resumé

I WAS A LONG, NARROW-SHOULDERED man with a briefcase that hung open and empty from my hand. I was stretched over the back of the post office bench, every part of me limp except for the hand clinging to the briefcase handle. My head hung back and my Adam's apple pointed at the sky. It was about four in the afternoon, hot, and no one else was on the street when the old woman found me. She gave me a tap with her walking stick to see if I was alive. I didn't move. She walked around me and tapped from the other side. Nothing. Then she gave my shins a good whack with the stick and that convinced her that I was dead. She tried to steal the briefcase, but it wouldn't come out of my hand. The old woman went away, muttering.

I was a long, narrow-shouldered man floating face-down in a swimming pool. The pool maintenance man found me when he pulled the cover back. I had obviously been in the water for a long time. I was swollen. The owners of the pool were questioned, but not detained. I carried no identification. The broken clasp of my briefcase was engraved with three initials. This detail was not given to the press.

I was a tall, narrow-shouldered man found hanging from a bridge. My noose had been constructed from a neck tie. One of the

103

coroner's assistants made a joke about that as he carried a tray of instruments into the room. The coroner might have thought the joke was funny, but he wasn't listening. He was trying to take the open briefcase from my hand.

I was a tall, narrow-shouldered man in the television studio audience. I didn't clap for the contestants when everyone else did. For one thing, the handle of the briefcase with the broken clasp was in my hand. For another, I was dead.

The Black Forest was dying. The trees stood stripped of needles like tall, narrow-shouldered men. One misty morning, a hiker noticed briefcases hanging from the branches. Each briefcase had a broken clasp, so they all hung open. Dew drops collected on the leather.

I was the lost father. I wandered everywhere looking for you, carrying inside my briefcase the photograph of the two of us together for the last time in 1964.

I was a tall, narrow-shouldered man asleep on the heating grate. Or so it seemed.

On the enemy beach, I washed ashore as planned. The enemy soldiers found me, found the obviously forged papers in my breast pocket. It was hoped that they would also force the lock on the briefcase that was chained to my hand and find the papers there, the photographs of beaches with landing zones marked in red. But the clasp had broken open in the waves. The briefcase was empty.

I was a tall, narrow-shouldered man discovered in a block of glacial ice. I was thawed out, and the contents of my stomach were analyzed. My diet had consisted partly of alpine flowers. The briefcase in my hand was not taken seriously.

I was a tall, narrow-shouldered man found twenty hours after the hijacking, the partly-opened parachute tangled by the wind amongst the sagebrush. The open briefcase in my hand held no trace of the hundred-thousand dollars. There were no recent tracks in the sand.

The coroner's assistant opened my drawer by mistake, pulled the sheet back from my face, and the woman cried, "That's him! That's my brother!" The assistant realized his mistake, but the woman insisted: "That's his briefcase! That was what he was carrying when he left home thirty years ago!" I was not as she remembered me, though. Now I was taller, narrower of shoulder. "I knew you when you were a baby," she told me.

I was a tall, narrow-shouldered man you met once at a party. You talked to me for a long time about Nicaragua. Then, six months later, you thought you saw me in a newspaper photograph of the war dead in Managua. The briefcase partly obscured my face.

I was a tall, narrow-shouldered man stretched out on the park bench, maybe dead, maybe asleep. There was a briefcase in my hand, a briefcase opened wide, and the papers inside were flying off with the wind, messages carried to anyone willing to receive them.

One Thing After Another

1.

One word follows another.

2.

Life is good for Brigit and Michael. Then one morning, mastodon bones erupt through the front lawn. Natural history people come. "These bones belong in a museum," says a woman with a clipboard. She gives Brigit a dirty look. Trucks and cranes arrive. When they leave, there is a hole big enough for a living mastodon to fall into. The possibility keeps Michael awake, listening to the dark.

3.

Getting older is bad enough. Hair in the nose, hair in the ears. But then cat fur starts to grow on the inside of Larry's mouth, too thick and fast-growing to shave. He develops an allergic wheeze. Worse, he can't get words to form with his furry tongue. It makes him angry. There was still a lot more he wanted to say.

4.

Nancy comes home from her job at the grief clinic. Her house is on fire. No one has to tell her that her husband and children were trapped inside. Some teenagers are leaning on their cars, watching the flames and listening to music. She walks over to them. She asks them to turn the music up. Then, partly to find out who she is now, she asks them, "Who wants to dance?"

5.

Once Gabriel decides about her, his concentration is shot. He calls her. He sends her notes with flowers. Things slide at work. He calls some more, sends more flowers. "All right," she says. After they make love for the first time, he notices that one of her teeth is not straight. It will not be the last thing he notices.

6.

Paul's technical manual about oil-rig fires went out of print thirty years ago. He is surprised to find a copy in the Loveland, Ohio, library, a thousand miles from home. Someone has highlighted passages. On the last page are a few lines of feminine handwriting in purple ink. "The author is afraid of death. He takes long walks alone at night, thinking of Rilke's angels. He is young, but already there are secrets he will take to his grave." When he looks up from reading, Paul doesn't really expect someone to be watching him. And no one is.

7.

First there's a word, then there's the next one. One after another. Another leaf drops. Drops of rain strike the window with a sound close to breathing. Breathing the same darkness, we hold each other. Other leaves will drop, other storms will shake down rain, other words will tumble out of us and we will come back to this place again and again hoping to find the one thing our bodies long for us to say. Say something else for now. Now say the thing you think of first.

Invasions

Invading the farm, we round up the livestock for questioning. Invading the grocery store check-out lanes, we hold ten or fewer items hostage. Invading Invasion headquarters, we make a guest appearance on the nightly news. The interviewer asks us what we're trying to accomplish. We say, "Invasions."

The drawbridge opens just after we've passed over. The railroad crossing barriers come down behind us when there is no train. Bright lights meant to illuminate us for the snipers refuse to shine in our direction. The time is right for these invasions. Everything is on our side.

Invading music, we organize the notes by duration: whole notes at the beginning of songs, sixteenths at the end. Invading the spectrum, we give microwaves the freedom to be as big as they want. Invading this sentence, syntax the scramble we.

Invading this paragraph, we capture the topic sentence, leaving the remaining sentences leaderless. The tribe's arrival in the valley had been preceded by two major displacements. That's what friends are for. Less commercially important, perhaps, is camphor. Uncanny is not quite the right term. Pull and release in a steady motion. Bump, bump, bump went the shoe as it tumbled down the stairs.

Invading your cat, we arm it and give it the means to carry off the plots it has plotted all along. Invading your old dog, we teach it new tricks. One of them is to tell you to get the hell off the couch, that's not a place for people.

Invading the kitchen, we teach the forks to loathe the spoons for their lazy roundness, the spoons to hate the knives for their edginess, the knives to distrust the forks for their inability to come to just one point. Utensils conspire against one another. How did that spoon end up in the garbage disposal? Who put these forks in the trash? How did this knife get bent unto a U?

Invading the opera, we force the fat lady to sing early. Invading the library, we judge books by their covers. Blue is good, but red is a sign of dangerous thoughts.

Invading the snack cake factory, we confiscate the creme filling and build a pyramid of golden sponge cake. At the top of this pyramid our priests will cut out the hearts of healthy people. We distribute the creme filling at schools and workplaces. Every citizen must eat a share, or else mount the golden steps.

Invading the taste buds, we see to it that lettuce and rose petals are indistinguishable except by their crunch. We teach roses to be crunchy.

Invading the weather service, we make our own forecasts. The weather tomorrow will be vanilla with touches of cumin and clove in the afternoon. Strong ginger overnight. The following day will be burlap changing to silk by evening. Look for brass Saturday and Sunday with a possible trace of woodwinds, changing to strings and percussion by Monday. The six-day extended outlook calls for seasonably loquacious days and above normal enunciation.

Justice is swift in the new order. If you can't sing the Invasion Anthem, you'd better make one up on the spot. We're not kidding.

Invading the schools, we look around and consider whether independent thought can survive such institutions. Are we in favor of independent thought? Which side are we on? We're still waiting for someone to tell us. In the meantime, we alter the curriculum so that future citizens will understand the meanings of Burma Shave and "They laughed when I sat down at the piano."

Invading the piano, we laugh whenever anyone sits down at it.

Invading sleep, we collect large fees for product placement in your dreams.

Invading the air, we become the biggest, bluest butterflies anyone has ever seen. Invading the oceans, we become finned serpents a mile long. Invading the cornfields, we become crows the size of eagles. Invading the swimming pool, we become sharks too small to be seen with the naked eye.

Invading the senior center, we alter all the Jimmy Dorsey records so that they sound more like Eddie Van Halen. Soon enough. Soon enough. Soon enough no one will be left who notices the change.

Invading the garbage trucks, we stop to marvel at how much perfectly good stuff people throw away. This toothbrush may smell bad, but it's hardly been used!

Invading the university, we reorganize the departments. No more Mechanical Engineering Department. No more English Department or Psychology Department. Now it's the Department of Things That Got Rhythm, the Department of Panhandler Studies, the Department of Mood Swing Engineering. Students must change their majors. Some will get their degrees in Enormity, Repetition, or Yellow Stuff Science. One or two will minor in Perturbation. A course in fortune telling will be required so that every graduate has something to fall back on.

Invading the commodities market, we halt trading to alter the nomenclature. After we're done, Free Love for September delivery opens a penny higher. December Humdingers are down the limit. March contracts on the Rolly Polly 500 are off by 27 points.

Invading the museums, we tie up the guards and impersonate great works of art.

Invading the homes of married couples, we wear our most elegant suits, our slinkiest gowns. We come bearing chocolate and flavored oils. We wear one velvet glove. We float in on a miasma of intoxicating scents. We awaken the passions that familiarity and routine have allowed to sleep. We teach passionate utterances in other tongues. "Comme ça. Oui. ¡Tan dulces tus cariños! Presto! Si! Presto! Presto!" And then we leave while the passions are hot and husbands and wives have nowhere to direct that heat but at one another.

Invading the airline industry, we ban airplanes and institute long-distance travel by balloon. If the wind won't carry you to your destination then you weren't meant to go there.

Invading chemistry, we provoke latent enmities between oxygen and hydrogen. Water breaks up. Life as we know it will have to change.

One day the invasion will be over. One day, we'll be gone. One day, you'll have to rely on your own resources. But until then, we're here. Until then, we're doing what we can.

Come the Revolution

WHEN NEAL MADE LOVE TO Deanna that night in October, the smell of rabbits was still with him: the mustiness of their fur and of the little pellets they left behind in the floor of the vans. The smell had been driving Neal into a frenzy as he steered the first van into the desert. With his sidelong glances at Deanna, he caught her sidelong glances at him. Yes, he had thought, tonight he would have her. The surveillance cameras, alarm systems, and electronic locks of the research lab had all fallen to her. Tonight she would fall to him.

Three identical white vans had followed his down the dirt roads and onto the wide open spaces. As Neal and the others released the rabbits into the desert, a gibbous moon rose out of the mountains. Neal had an almost painful erection. He said as he opened the cages and released the laboratory rabbits into the wild, "You are free! Free! Free!"

Now, back in his apartment, he repeated the words as he gripped Deanna's wide hips. "Free! Free!" He was Pappa Bunny doing Momma Bunny. Deanna trembled as he collapsed against her, as he lay down beside her, as he turned her face and kissed her tears that he hoped were tears of passion.

Then he smelled her hair. "Is that White Rain conditioner?" he said.

He knew before she clutched him and sobbed "Yes!" that it *was* White Rain. He'd led a raid on the manufacturer, spilling hundreds of gallons of their product from the mixing vats. He'd been caught. He'd done time for that raid. The stench of White Rain would never fully fade from memory. "Deanna!" he said. "Gillette makes that! They test with animals!"

"I know! I know!" she cried against his neck. "I can't live a lie any longer! Neal, I'm not who you think I am. I'm not one of you!"

"What do you mean?" He pushed her away so he could look into her tearful eyes. "You've gotten us into the labs. We've freed chimps and rabbits and white mice together. We've turned loose monkeys and lab rats from labs with the highest security, all thanks to you. Of course you're one of us!"

"Neal, you've been so blind! All you think about is animal rights! Haven't you ever had a single thought about animal wrongs?"

"What are you talking about?"

"I'm talking about the destructive power of termites and the viciousness of yellowjackets. I'm talking about herbivores that would denude the earth if they could get away with it. I'm talking about bloodthirsty carnivores. I'm talking about animal respiration and digestion, the unending production of CO_2 and methane. I'm talking about mucous secretions and bad smells. Animals, Neal. Animals are *wrong*!"

"But Deanna. *We're* animals."

"That is disgustingly and inescapably true. But that doesn't make it right."

He couldn't believe what he was hearing. "But you've gotten us past all the security, helped us to liberate countless—"

"Liberate? Neal, we used you. Don't you read the papers? The animals that don't die of dehydration on the desert are shot. And who do you think does the shooting?"

"But those stories are all propaganda. The same people that

control the research labs control the press."

"No. Those stories are the truth. We get you to bring out the animals. You drop them off in the desert where our snipers can pick them off in the moonlight."

"Why are you telling me this? I refuse to believe it!"

She held his face in her hands. "Believe it, Neal!" She kissed him. "Believe it! There's no future in animal rights. Join us!"

When Neal tried to mount Deanna that night in May, the smell of ponies was still with him: the oaty tang of their breath, the rich mustiness of their stalls. How nervously they had stamped their feet before Deanna raised the muzzle of her gun to their heads. The smells, the fear, the muzzle flashes in the dark of the petting zoo had driven Neal into a frenzy as he, Deanna and the others made their way from goats to piglets to chickens and ponies. The operation took under five minutes, and the three black vans were vanishing into the night long before the sheriff's deputies arrived. As Neal drove, his sidelong glaces at Deanna had caught her sidelong glances at him. Yes, he had thought, tonight he would have her again. Finally.

But now she resisted as he tried to press her down onto her leather couch. She pushed him away. "No, we can't. We mustn't. It's so *animal!*"

She cried. He let her up. It wasn't that she didn't love him, he knew, but that she had become more and more radical, more committed, with every passing day. No matter how many animals the Animal Extermination Front destroyed, there were always more born the next day. How could they have sex without thinking of the ghastly fecundity of their enemy?

"You're right," he said, gritting his teeth. "We're better than that."

Disgusted, he put his leather pants back on, then his leather shirt, his leather jacket, his leather shoes with the leather laces. As he slammed the front door behind him and dragged his shoes along the front walk, he didn't know which was worse, his sexual frustration or the depressing thought that even if he wore out a new pair of leather shoes every day, he would barely make a dent in the total cow population. He lit a cigarette with his leather-shelled lighter and walked the streets, under the moon.

He had intended to be a double agent, to *pretend* to believe in animal wrongs while staying in touch with his former compatriots in animal rights. But the simple truth was that as soon as he'd killed a few times to prove himself trustworthy, he'd started to like it. He had started to loathe animals. They were, when you got right down to it, easy to hate.

As Neal walked around a corner, engines roared. Tires screeched. White light flared around Neal. He raised his hand against the sudden glare of searchlights on three sides.

"Hold it!" a voice said.

"Jeez," said another. "It *is* him! And he's wearing leather!"

He knew the voices. Old comrades. He could barely make out the shapes of white vans beneath the lights. "Wait!" he said. "I can explain!" Two of them were behind him in an instant, pressing a chloroform-soaked rag against his nose and mouth. "Deanna!" he cried.

Neal's re-education process had been straightforward. Dr. Andrea Windover, past-life regression therapist and animal rights sympathizer, had given Neal two drugs. One grew hair all over his body. The other drug made him susceptible to deep hypnosis. When Dr. Andrea had made sure that Neal was deeply, deeply relaxed, she said, "You are remembering the life before this one." When he could remember it in some detail, she said, "Now you are going back to the life before that one." Later: "Now the life before that." And once he had the hang of it, she didn't need to pause between lives. "Now the life before that. Now the life before that.

116

Now the life before that. Before that. Before that."

Back, back, back. Deeper and deeper into the past she had taken him, back to the days of Australopithecus. When he woke up after weeks of intensive regression, his arms seemed longer to him. When he felt his forehead, it seemed to slope. He wasn't sure what was real and what was merely the result of powerful hypnotic suggestion. Certainly, the thick black hair all over his body was real.

"You *are* an animal," the regression therapist said. "You have always been an animal, remember?"

Neal had wept salty animal tears.

Now as he made his way into the laboratory, dragging his hairy knuckles lightly along the floor, Neal was overwhelmed with sadness, both for the chimps he could smell in their cages, and for his separation from Deanna. "You're sure the alarms were all disabled?" he said to his companions.

"Got it," one of them said, giving him a thumbs up. But Neal was nervous. If Deanna were here, he could have relied on her to get through security. She'd have done it for him, done it for love, even if she couldn't be trusted to know the details of their plans. These chimps would be disguised as retirees for the border crossing and driven down to the jungles of southern Mexico, where they could live nearly natural lives. But Deanna had gone deep underground after Neal was snatched. Neal had no idea where she might be.

Neal picked the lock on the lab door. "Ooh-ooh," he said soothingly to the chimps in their wire cages. "Ooh-ooh."

As the Animal Liberation Front loaded the locked wire cages into moonlit white vans, the first six squad cars appeared, red and blue lights flashing. "Break the hinges!" Neal shouted. Neal hurried to pry open two of the cages himself. Then with all the liberated chimps, he dodged between cop cars and into the shadows of surrounding buildings.

"You must hate animals," Neal said to the researcher as her young assistant unlocked the laboratory cage and led him out. The assistant dug into his Neal's with her fingernails. Neal had resisted before. She was reminding him, he thought, that resistance would bring pain. He let her guide him away from the cages to the chair.

"To the contrary," said the scientist, a woman with gray hair and a syringe in one hand. She was writing something in a notebook with her other hand. "I love animals. I have two cats and a dog at home."

The assistant pushed Neal down into the chair and adjusted the arm straps. Then, when he was fully restrained, she pinched his arm.

"Ow!" Neal said.

"Are the straps uncomfortable?" the scientist asked, looking up.

"She, um..." Neal looked at the assistant. She was glaring. She was the one who fed him and changed his water. Or 'forgot' to feed him. "It's nothing."

The scientist swabbed the shaved spot on his arm and injected something.

"I'm not a chimp," Neal said. "I don't think I'm even really an Australopithecus."

"Sometimes one must maintain a fiction," the scientist said, "for the sake of science. I'm sure the police understood when they handed you over that you weren't like the others. But under the circumstances..."

The circumstances had been that one of the escaping chimps had been run over by a late-arriving police cruiser. The laboratory needed eight chimpanzees for the study. After the liberation raid, one of the eight was dead.

Neal looked again at the cramped cages, including the one he'd just come from. "I do think you hate animals," he said.

"This research will save human lives one day," said the scientist. "I don't hate animals. I don't think, as *some* people seem to, that human lives are worth sacrificing for the comfort of animals. Between the people haters and the animal haters, I think they're both crazy."

"But what about me? How can you do these things to me?" Neal said. The research assistant lowered a hood over his face. He felt the brace against his skull. The brace tightened as the assistant locked it into position. "It's not the shocks today, is it?" He felt the back of the hood open, felt the cold jelly of the electrodes. "I really don't like the shocks."

"I'm afraid it *is* the shocks today," said the scientist. "Sorry."

"I am a human being!" Neal shouted. "I have rights! Human or animal, I have rights!"

The assistant pinched the back of his neck. Hard. It hurt. He whimpered. But what he said was, "I don't like the shocks."

Later, when Neal lay dazed at the bottom of the cage, he thought he saw Deanna's face on the other side of the wire. Her lips were parted. She said, "Do you want out of here?"

"I do," Neal whispered. He blinked. Something was wrong with Deanna's face. He blinked again. She wasn't Deanna. She was the assistant.

"If you want out of here," she said very softly, "then disable the alarm tonight." She pointed to the wall. "Turn the red key to off. We'll come for you."

Neal clutched the wire cage. "How will I—"

"The lock of your cage is in its hasp. But it's not locked. You can let yourself out."

"Why would you—"

"Shh. Explanations later."

Before him was the star-lit desert. Flat. Stony. There was no vegetation to speak of, nothing that would provide cover. He shivered and turned back toward the three women standing before their van. They had given him some kind of drug, something that made him dizzy and made his eyes teary, so now these women with their rifles seemed to be underwater.

"Run!" said the assistant.

"Why?"

"To make it more sporting," said one of the others. "Run!"

They had come to the lab after midnight. He had opened the door when he heard them. They had shoved him back into his cage and hauled the cage out to their van. A red van. For rescuers, they didn't treat him very gently. Everybody hates somebody, he thought. He said, afraid that he already knew, "Who do you hate?"

They laughed. "You!" one of them said.

"Activists," the assistant added. "We hate political activists."

He thought about that. Was he an activist, or a spy, or a double-agent? "But I don't even know what side I'm on any more!"

"Doesn't matter! Doesn't matter one bit! Animal rights! Animal wrongs! Abortion rights! Right to life! Rights of the accused! Victims' rights! We hate 'em all the same."

Now, as the women told him one more time to run or to be shot where he stood, he thought of Deanna. Maybe she'd had a change of heart. Awkwardly, stumbling over ground that felt spongy to his drugged legs, falling and then getting up again, he thought that Deanna could have changed sides. He had changed for her, hadn't he? Maybe she'd been keeping track of him. Maybe she had changed for *him*. Maybe the two of them were their own side. Just the two of them.

A rifle cracked and a ricochet sang its weird note.

Maybe Deanna was riding to the rescue even now, he thought. And then, yes, he saw her coming. He saw a white van, brilliant, approaching from the east, rising.

It was the moon.

A Story For Discussion

WHEN THE AUTHOR AWOKE from troubled dreams one morning, he found that he had been transformed in his bed into an enormous abstraction. He was accustomed to waking up with sore wrists from the previous day's typing, a headache from the previous evening's red wine, and an aching back from the night's lumpy mattress. On this morning he had no bodily complaints of any kind. He had no body. He rose from the bed and looked around to make sure. There was no sign of the body that he'd gone to sleep in. It wasn't there in the bedclothes. It wasn't under the bed.

The author wondered if his body might be hiding in some other room of the house, or in some other house in the neighborhood. Suddenly, he found himself rising as if in an invisible elevator — up through the ceiling of his bedroom, past the attic, through the roof of his house, high into the sky. As he rose higher and higher, he was surprised to find that he saw things below him in greater and greater detail. He could see not only the roofs of a dozen, of a hundred, of a thousand houses, but he could make out the individual grains on each shingle. And he saw *through* roofs. He saw through walls. In apartments and houses, he could see anything he thought to look for. He could see where every set of keys was, for example: in pockets, in purses, on dressers, hanging from ignition switches, lost in high grass or in storm sewers.

What he didn't see, not anywhere in the city or anywhere in the world, was his body.

There were other bodies that he could see, twining on rumpled sheets on motel beds, on couches. Even this early in the morning, there were two teenagers making a van rock gently in the high school parking lot. The boy's name was Larry. The girl's was Crystal. The author listened to what Larry whispered in Crystal's ear. Nothing special. Just, "I love you" over and over. The author knew that Crystal shouldn't rely too much on what Larry was saying at the moment, but he couldn't say whether she knew that or not. Wait. Actually, he could say. Yes, to some degree she knew that Larry's declaration was suspect, but Crystal chose to believe it anyway. Her father had abandoned her mother long ago. She wanted to believe. She wanted to be loved. She wanted to be better than her mother at holding onto a man.

The author knew that what Larry wanted was much simpler, particularly at the moment. In a few weeks, however, everything in both of their lives would be far more complicated.

The author felt a faint twinge of guilt over his voyeurism, seeing these young people so clearly and intimately in both the present and the future, but he reminded himself that he was, after all, an author. Everything was research.

Larry's muscles tensed, and the boy's bodily sensations reminded the author that he had been searching for his own body. He returned his attention to his own house.

He searched attic, bedroom, and bathroom again. He looked in the closets. He turned his attention to the downstairs rooms, and he noticed something he had not seen before. Something strange. There were people gathered in his kitchen. A gray-haired man was making pancakes in the author's own house, and a somewhat younger blonde woman was serving those pancakes to much younger men and women who were gathered around the dining room table or were seated on the floor. Who were these people? He didn't know. He couldn't imagine what they were thinking. Why were they opaque to him, unlike Larry and Crystal?

The gray-haired man flipped the last of the pancakes and untied his apron. Raising his voice so that he could be heard in the dining room, he said, "The first line of this story parallels the beginning of a famous story."

One of the young people raised his hand. When the blonde woman called on him, he said "Kafka. The Metamorphosis."

The older man came in from the kitchen carrying two bar stools. He sat on one. The blonde woman sat on the other. "The Metamorphosis. What do you make of that?"

"Allusion. He wants us to think of that story."

"Because?"

No one said anything. Then one young woman with dark skin and eyes quietly asked someone to pass the syrup.

The blonde woman asked, "What do we learn from the author's description of his customary aches and pains?"

"That he's a hack," said the same young man who had spoken earlier. "He drinks. He writes so much every day that his wrists ache. If you write that much, you can't be thinking about what you're writing."

"He doesn't have to be a hack," said a thin young woman who hadn't touched her pancakes.

"He isn't a hack," said a young man with a wispy beard. "He drinks red wine. A hack would drink beer or whisky."

"Both," said another student. "Whisky and a beer chaser."

"What?" scoffed the young man who thought the author was a hack. "You don't think that writers of trashy novels might drink red wine?"

"Not in fiction," said the thin woman. "In fiction every detail is a signifier."

"I wish there wasn't any alcohol at all," said the dark-eyed woman. "You don't have to drink to write. I'm a writer, and I don't drink."

The young man who thought the author must be a hack raised his eyebrows. "Published anything?"

She glared. "What's your point?"

"We're drifting a bit from the matter at hand," said the gray-haired man. "The author is said to have become an abstraction. What kind of abstraction?"

"Point of view."

"Omniscient point of view."

"No," said the young man who talked the most. "Limited omniscient. He sees inside of Crystal's head, but not Larry's."

"That's just because there's not much in Larry's head to report," said the dark-eyed woman.

"Well, wait a minute," said the young man with the beard. "The author characterizes Larry's motivation. 'What Larry wanted was much simpler, particularly at the moment.' That reports Larry's subjective experience. Omniscient."

"But this supposedly omniscient point of view," said the dark-eyed woman, "didn't see us sitting here in the author's dining room. Not initially."

The thin woman said, "I don't think it matters what kind of abstraction. I think the point—"

"Where is the author now?" said a student who hadn't spoken before. "He was right here in the beginning, and now we haven't heard from him. Is he even in the story any more?"

They looked around.

The thin woman who still hadn't touched her pancakes began to stack plates, preparing to clear the table.

The gray-haired man looked at his watch, then looked meaningfully at the blonde woman.

"Right, then," she said. "That's it for today. For next time, bring us one paragraph on what you think is the principal purpose of this story."

"Double-spaced," he reminded them.

He looked at her. She at him. And they took it as a confirmation of their dreams and good intentions when, at the end of the hour, the students stood up and stretched their young bodies.

IV. Tales

The Djinn Who Lives Between Night and Day

THE DJINN AL-FAQ LIVED in the crack between night and day. He rarely ventured out into the worlds of his fellow djinn, much less into the world of mortal men. No one but God and Al-faq himself knew whether or not he was a faithful djinn, so the obedient sprits and disobedient alike thought of him as one of their own. Djinn of both kinds visited Al-faq to tell him their stories.

Tayab, the djinn of ashes, came to the crack between night and day. Laughing, he called out, "Cousin! I have such a story to tell you!"

"What have you done now, Tayab?"

The djinn of ashes only laughed some more, so Al-faq said, "Well, come in, cousin, and have some tea. You must tell me your tale from the beginning."

When the tea was brewed, Tayab said, "Do you know the people of the red desert? The ones who live along the river?"

Al-faq gave no answer but nodded for Tayab to continue.

"The plague came to them," said the djinn of ashes. "Every house had its dead. You never heard such wailing! That was what drew me, cousin. The anguish of the living. All those lamentations carried on the wind...I know an opportunity when I hear one!"

Al-faq said, "Go on."

"From one house, I heard shrieks more terrible than all the rest. There a woman was tearing at her clothes, pulling out her hair. Her husband tried to hold her hands at her sides. He was crying, too, but not like her. His face was wet, but he was silent. Her arms and his were bloodied where she had scratched them. And her keening! Oh, I have seldom heard grief like hers. It was delicious," Tayab said, "because I was sure I could make something of it."

"Some mischief," said Al-faq. He sipped his tea.

"Better than mere mischief," said Tayab. "Now, listen. I sniffed around their house, and in seven places I found the shadow of the dark angel. Seven times during the plague he had entered and taken a soul. Children, I guessed. This woman had borne seven children, and now all of them were dead. When she was too spent to cry out, she whispered their names." He told Al-faq what the names of the children had been. "Her husband tried to comfort her. Useless. He said her name, and she would not answer. When he tried to meet her gaze, she turned away."

"His grief must have been as great."

"Perhaps, perhaps. Who can tell when they aren't loud like her, when they don't rend their clothes? So I waited until he was asleep. Her eyes were still wide open, though it was too dark for her to see. I knelt over her and I whispered, 'Mortal woman, I am the angel of the gate, and I have heard your prayers.'"

"The angel of the gate?" said Al-faq.

"It's nothing. I made it up. But I said to her, 'I will return your children to life if you will but keep faith with me.'"

"And if an angel hears of this?"

"But I didn't take the name of any angel, cousin. Didn't I just say that I made it up? I said to the woman, 'Get up. Go out. Walk west. Go until you can go no farther. I will give you a sign that your children have returned, but you must stay there by the sea, alone, with nothing. You must never speak again. You must never seek your children, for if you find one then all seven must die.'"

"And she agreed to this bargain?"

"She did! She got up without waking her husband. She took only the clothes she wore, and she walked! Day and night she walked! Out of the desert and over the mountains, all the way to the sea!"

"And you? Did you return her children to life?"

Tayab laughed. "Return them to life?" He held his sides and laughed some more. "Well, I did what I could, cousin. I did all that it was in my power to do. I came to her in the night and told her to look to the eastern sky. Stars fell from the heavens, and as each one fell, I gave it the name of one of her children."

"She believed you."

"Far better than believed me, cousin, and that is the sugar in the tea! I left her. And when I returned the next night, there she was within sight of the waves, sheltering in a cave in the cliffs! I said, 'Now, listen, mortal woman. I am no angel. I am a djinn. As for you, I have never met a greater fool, for I can no more restore your children to life that I can make the sun rise in the west. You don't need to stay here and starve beside the sea. Go home, now. Go home!'"

"And did she?"

"That's the wonder!" The djinn of ashes laughed once more. "She would not answer me, for I had told her that she must not speak. And she would not believe me, for I had told her that she must keep faith with the angel of the gate. So there she stayed, wordless, friendless, with only a cave for shelter, steady in her faith in a divine servant that does not exist!"

"But *you* exist, cousin."

"I do, to be sure," said Tayab with a grin.

"And did she starve?"

"Villagers by the sea found her. They bring her food. They think she is a holy woman." He laughed again.

"And what of her husband?"

"That's not my story, cousin. He still lives, I suppose, if he has not died yet."

"I wonder about him."

Tayab waved the thought away. "But what do you think? I took everything from her, even more than I intended! And now even if I try to return what I stole, she won't take it! Have you ever heard of thievery such as mine?"

Al-faq stroked his face with his long fingers and gave no answer. Perhaps Tayab expected none.

When the djinn of ashes had gone, Al-faq left his home in the crack between night and day. He went to the world of mortal men. It took him a long time to find the red desert and even longer to find the house with seven now fading shadows. The fields next to the house was overgrown. The man who lived there was hollow-eyed and thin.

Al-faq waited for nightfall. When at last the man fell into his bed, he moaned his wife's name. Al-faq leaned close in the darkness and said, "'Mortal man, I am the angel of the gate, and I have heard your prayers. As you feared, your wife, like your children, is dead. I will return them all to life if you will but keep faith with me."

"Yes?" said the man. "You can do this?"

"Get up," said Al-faq. "Go out. Walk south. Walk until you can go no farther. I will give you a sign that your wife and children have returned to life, but you must stay there by the sea, alone, with nothing. You must never speak again. You must never seek the ones you love, for if you find one, then all eight must die."

The man got up. He threw on his clothes. He took up his walking stick and set out at once. Through the night he walked. He walked through the next day. In time, he crossed the desert. In time, he crossed the plains. Al-faq, invisible, came behind him. When the man had walked all the way to the sea, the djinn waited for nightfall and then showed him eight falling stars in the northern sky. To each falling star, Al-faq gave a name.

"Remember," said the djinn. "Never speak. Never look for them."

The man's face was wet with tears. He nodded.

"Keep faith with me always, no matter what."

The man nodded again and smiled wearily. He made a gesture of gratitude, of blessing.

"No, do not bless me," said Al-faq. "I am not worthy."

At the nearest village, the djinn went from house to house and whispered in the ears of many sleepers: "There is a holy man beside the sea. Find him. Care for him."

Then the djinn Al-faq, who perhaps is a faithful djinn and perhaps is not, returned to the crack between night and day. And if the world has not yet ended, he lives there still.

Listening, Listening

ANYONE WHO SANG OUT sweet and high over the waters of the lake might bring up the monster if the light and air were right, but none of the men living in those rough cabins were willing to sing out in a voice like a woman's, and they weren't about to let their women do it, either. No, they would say, whatever is meant to be seen will appear of its own accord and will rise when it is meant to rise. What lies in our keeping is the fruit of our traplines: the fox, the hare, the mink. If our roofs were beneath the lake, our traps would be there, too. We will not disturb the sleep of anything we don't mean to kill.

So the women met by night, slipping from the sides of sleeping husbands when moon and mists were as they had to be. They gathered on the rock that rose, shiplike, from the farthest shore, and they held their breaths to hear the sound of coils unwinding underneath the waves. Then some one of them would softly sing a note as clear as water, and another voice would join hers, and another after that. The men, still asleep in their beds, would dream of masts and sirens.

Sometimes a shadow would glide beneath the surface. Sometimes not. Sometimes the waves would clash with ripples that rose up from below. Sometimes not. And then on some rare nights, the monster, dripping water from its nostrils, would raise its head into the glowing mist to listen to the one-note song.

And then the giant head would slip back beneath the waves. The steady song would slip back into silence. The women, silently, would slip between black trees, back to their cabins, back beside their husbands.

Among themselves again in daylight, the women would exchange no glance, speak no secret word about what passed in the night, even after the men, with traps and chains rattling from their shoulders, had made their way into the shadows of the trees.

Once a man who dreamed of sirens reached for his wife and, not finding her, woke up. He rose, naked, and followed the sound, the one high note in many voices, until he came to the water's edge. Out across the lake, he saw the women singing, saw the water ripple underneath the moon.

The moonlight shone whitely on his body, and he let the cold air in through his nose and out through his mouth. And then, without meaning to, he lifted up his voice, singing with the voice of a woman from the body of a man.

The water did not froth in the center of the lake. The great head did not rise into the mist. At last, one by one, the women fell silent, until the man was the last one singing. He stayed there on the rocky shore, sending his voice out over the water long after the women, even his wife, had made their way back to their beds. When he stopped singing, he crouched beside the water, unable to go home. When the eastern sky began to pink, his nakedness drove him back.

His wife was waiting up. She had a fire in the stove, and she looked at him strangely when he came in.

He stood confounded for a moment, and then he lowered his brow. "What was that nonsense you were up to last night?" he demanded. Then he put on his clothes. "I can't look at you, woman," he said. "I'm ashamed of the things you do. I am so ashamed."

He never spoke of it to her again, but some nights he would

wake to the sound of singing. He would not stretch out to feel the bed empty beside him, but would lie very still and angry, imagining what it looked like, the massive head held high above the water, listening, listening.

The Rower

ONCE UPON A TIME there was a young woman who meant to drown herself. So many sorrows had come to her that she decided her grief was too much to bear. The day had not yet come that was the right day for drowning. But it would come. So she stayed in a hut in a village by the sea. She waited.

A storm came up on the shortest day of the year. She had seen great storms before, but this one was different. The rain struck the houses like arrows shooting between the timbers. Again and again, the wind blew open doors and windows that had been lashed shut. Roofs peeled away. In the village, people shivered under their beds, cold and wet and waiting for the storm to end as light faded from the day.

The woman in the hut by the edge of the sea was not under her bed. She had gone down to the water, where the waves smashed themselves upon the rocks. Her head was bent low against the rain and spume. She was listening. She was smelling the cold air. Yet it wasn't sound or smell that told her what her heart knew. Something about this storm was different from all the other storms she had ever known. There was sorrow in this dark wind. In the heart of the storm was a pain like her own.

The boats were tied down beyond the reach of the storm tide, but she freed one and dragged it to the water. The waves nearly broke the boat against the rocks, but the woman got her oars into the locks and rowed into the dark, pulling against both wind and wave. Bit by bit, she rowed away from the shore.

As she rowed, the storm grew even more violent. The waves were as tall as haystacks on either side of her, but still she rowed. At length, the waves diminished. The wind settled, then suddenly died. The sky overhead cleared, though she saw the stars glow red, as if through smoke. In the center of this stillness was a green light the like of which she had never seen before. She rowed toward it.

She paused to rest and to look at what she was rowing for. She could make out a lantern bobbing on the waves, and then the boat on which the lantern hung. It was a rowboat.

She rowed closer and looked again. She'd never seen a boat like this one before, fashioned with curls and knobs and flourishes of carving. The wood gleamed black in the lamp's strange light, and a figure pulled at the oars, following the coast as the storm had done.

When she lifted her oars again they creaked in the locks, and the figure froze. He stood up. He watched her.

She rowed closer. Her heart pounded, but she reminded herself that she had come to die. What could she fear?

His garments were tattered. His skin was gray, and stretched over his ribs as if he'd been nourished by nothing but rain drops for a long, long time. In the lantern's green glare, his eyes shone red as if with a light of their own.

"You are not him," he said in a voice that rolled in her ears like wind. "You are not the one I seek."

Her grief had long since made her bold. "Who are you?" she asked him.

"I am the one he made when the world was new."

"Who do you seek?"

"The one who made the world."

She asked him why.

He told her that when God had made the world, He had seen at once that sorrow was part of it. Indeed, pain had made the world as much as light had made the world. To make a world was to both begin and end with sadness. Oh, there was love, too. There was beauty. But love and beauty did not diminish sorrow. Sometimes, they increased the pain. And God did not desire to take all knowledge of this upon himself.

"So he made me," said the Rower. "As you, child, are made in God's image, I am made in the image of his pain. I will endure until the end of time, unless I can find him, unless I can make him take me back into himself. But though he is everywhere, he is never where I seek."

Her boat drifted so near that she could look into his eyes as she might look into a lover's. He held her gaze, unblinking. She dared to hold his gaze in return. The red glow of his eyes was the fire of stars burning through all time.

"I am alone," she said, "and grieving."

"You will die of grief sooner or later," he said. "That is how you were made." With that he went back to his oars and rowed out to sea, taking the storm with him. As he went, she saw that the stern of his boat bristled with thorns. As he went, the storm came up around her again.

The waves rolled and pitched the woman's little boat, but she did not sink. She rowed herself ashore and hauled the boat up to where she had taken it from. Before dawn broke, she had left that place by the sea.

She went to a country far inland. Among different people, she took up life again. She fell in love again, had children, and kept a garden where she grew hawthorn and thistle, roses and blackberries...anything with prickles and thorns.

Half of the Empire

A YOUNG MAN FROM A fishing village once went to the Capital to see what he would see. He left his little boat hove up on stony ground beneath the docks, and he gave no thought to the possibility that someone might steal it. He wandered the streets from the fish market to the workshops and foundries, on toward the farm markets and dry markets. The smells of vendors roasting nuts or searing meats made his mouth water, but he had no money. He had only salted fish in his pouch, and after he ate that he was still hungry. Although his stomach growled, he savored the smells more than most men with money would have enjoyed the tastes.

As he went farther and farther from the sea, he marveled at the clothes that grew finer and finer and the manners that were more and more refined until he scarcely knew his own countrymen. He kept going as the streets widened and led into the hills toward the marvelous white palace, which he stood before and admired for a time. The sun sank low in the sky, and a haze settled over the city. When the young man looked back at the way he had come, he could not see the sea.

As night fell, golden lanterns glowed on the streets. The paper windows of the houses were lit from within. There was no beauty like this in his village, though his village was comfortable enough and had a homely beauty of its own. He had planned to sleep beneath his boat, but with no waves beneath his feet and the stars hidden from view, he had turned so many times that now he had lost his way.

He knocked at a door, thinking that he would ask his way to the docks. He forgot what he meant to say, though, when the woman who answered was the most beautiful he had ever seen. For all her beauty, she looked sad, and her eyes were red as if from crying. Though she appeared to be no older than he was, she met his stare, and when he did not speak she said, "Why have you come?"

The young man said, "To, ah, to see...the master of the house."

"You will regret it," the woman said. She began to weep. "You should turn around and go right back the way you came."

"But I can't," the young man said.

"Because you are so very brave," the woman said. "I know."

"Bravery has nothing to do with it," the young man said. "I'm lost is all."

The woman's weeping ceased. She looked surprised. Indeed, she would have looked no more surprised if the young man had suddenly turned himself into an eel. "No one has ever said that before." Then she frowned. "But you aren't prepared. You're empty handed and perhaps empty headed as well. Are you sure you want to see the master?"

"I am sure."

She led him down a corridor and to a screen. Then she withdrew. As she went away, he could hear her weeping again. "She seems to have sorrows and worries aplenty," the young man said. "I wish I could do something for her." Then he slid the screen aside and stepped into the room behind it.

In the middle of the room sat a giant roasting meat over a brazier. He wore armor and two swords. When he saw the young man, he stood up, unsheathed the longer sword and said, "Why have you come?"

"To see the master of the house. Are you him?"

"I am the master's captain, and to see him, you must come through me. Prepare yourself."

The young man said, "If I have to fight you in order to see the master, I might as well pass the night here instead. It's warm with the brazier burning." The meat sizzled and smoked, and the young man's stomach growled.

"But haven't you come to see the master?"

"To tell you the truth, it's only by chance that I came here. I wanted to see the city, and now that I have seen it, I am ready to go home. But I got lost. When I came to the door, the woman who answered was so beautiful that I forgot what I had meant to say and asked to see the master. That woman is as sad as she is pretty. Do you know why?"

"She weeps for the men who come seeking to claim her. They all die in this room at my sword."

"And have many such men come?"

"Dozens and dozens for years and years."

"I see why she's sad. They must love her very much."

"It's the power they want, for her dowry is half the Empire."

"She's a princess, then?"

"I am surprised that you hadn't heard."

"I'm not from around here," said the young man. "Will you tell me the story?"

The giant lowered his sword. He and the young man sat on either side of the brazier, and the giant told how the princess had been enchanted by the master, who was a powerful sorcerer. She had not aged, but neither had she loved. Several times a year young men from the great cities of the empire came to win her, even though every suitor before them had died.

"She *is* very pretty," the young man said, "but at the moment the thing I am most interested in is getting something to eat and having a warm place to sleep."

"This is quite irregular," said the giant, "but since you didn't really come to fight me, I suppose it would be all right if you stayed as my guest." He drew the shorter sword and used it to cut the meat from the bone, and he gave a portion to the young man. They ate, then sat talking into the night about how to fight with a sword and how to cast a net. "Ah, how this makes me long for my soldiering life," the giant said, "when we would drink wine and talk like brothers, knowing that we might die the next day."

"That's not so different from life in my village," the young man said, "where we drink rice wine by the fire, and the next day one of us may drown." They spoke of wines, then, of which were better, the dry ones of rice or the sweet ones of fruit. The talk of wine made them as drowsy as a drink of wine might have done. At long last, they both fell asleep.

The coals in the brazier burned themselves out. The room grew cold, and the young man woke with the shivers. The giant snored. The cold seemed not to bother him at all. The young man thought that rather than waking the giant, he would see if he could find some more charcoal himself. He slid open the screen to the next room, which was not really a room at all, but a corridor like the one the woman had led him through. At the far end another screen glowed dimly.

"How strange this place is," the young man said to himself. "In my village, we build the rooms of a house next to one another." He walked down the corridor and opened the screen at the other end. The room he stepped into was very large, with wooden shelves lining the walls everywhere except for the place where he had just come in and a screen on the other side. Books and scrolls were stacked on the shelves, and they rose toward a ceiling so high that the young man couldn't see it in the darkness. The books might have gone up forever.

In the center of the room was a table where a bald man with a long white beard sat reading by the light of a candle. The young man crossed the room, and stood before the table. The white-haired man did not look up. He rubbed his temples as he read.

"Are you the master?" the young man said.

The old man looked up with a start. "You're here!" he said. "No one has ever come this far!" He patted himself as if to see if he were dreaming. "The master? No, I'm not the master. I'm his librarian, and I hadn't expected you. I haven't read quite all of them yet."

"I'd like some charcoal. The brazier has gone out," the young man explained.

"Brazier? That's of no importance. You've come to the library seeking the secret of the maze. Let me see, now. Which riddle shall I ask you?" He carried the candle to one of the shelves and squinted as he held the flame close to the bindings. He groaned. "The ink fades every year. It gets harder and harder to read these."

"Perhaps the brazier doesn't matter to you," the young man said, "but I'm quite cold sleeping in the other room."

"Pay no attention to the cold," the librarian said. "If you're to see the master, it's the mind that matters. What a man wants is knowledge and a sharp wit."

"What I want is fuel," the young man said. "Or a blanket."

The librarian was about to take a scroll from the shelf, then stopped and looked at the young man. "From the provinces. Ho! I know the one. You'll never get it." He crossed the room and selected a book. The binding was tied closed, and the old man was some time plucking at the string with his fingernails. At last he loosened the knot and opened the book. He squinted at the page, rubbing his temples again. "How my head aches. If only the candle burned a little brighter."

"I don't mind riddles," the young man said, "but what I really want..."

"Solve the riddle and you'll see the master," said the librarian, "and the master will give you your heart's desire. Now listen." He bent very close to the page until his nose almost touched. "The marks are so very faint. Hardly there at all. 'I proceed until I am no more, but there I am behind me once again.'"

The young man thought a moment and said, "A wave."

"No!" the librarian said. "It's the Emperor."

"Are you sure?" the young man said. "Is that what's in the book?"

The librarian looked at the page again. "To tell the truth, I can't make it out, but I am sure I remember this one. It's the Emperor."

"But a wave is just as good an answer. Where I come from, it's a better answer because we see waves every day, but we've never seen the Emperor."

The librarian frowned. "I picked this one because of course you haven't seen the Emperor. It's supposed to be hard." He stroked his beard. "But I suppose you are right. Not all wit or learning are already in books. Some of it still needs thinking up and writing down. I could write in the character for 'wave,' and then that would be the right answer and I could tell you how to pass the maze." And that is what he did.

The young man opened the screen and went through the branching corridors according to the librarian's directions. The corridors branched and turned, turned and branched. The young man came at last to another screen. He opened it, and there in the center of a large room, a brazier burned with a yellow flame. Next to the brazier was a pile of charcoal. A great heap of treasure gleamed in the firelight. There were rings and swords, a robe suitable for an Emperor, coins and pearls, boxes of jewels. There were other, more common things as well: a lamp, a mirror, a silken kerchief and a jar of wine.

The flame grew brighter, and a voice from within it spoke and said, "Take what you will."

The young man filled a sack with charcoal. Then he took up the lamp, the kerchief and the wine. To the flame he said, "How do I find my way to the docks beside the fish market?"

The flame told him the way to take. Then the young man retraced his steps. He left the lamp with the librarian, who lit it and found that it burned very bright indeed. How it would relieve his aching head! In the captain's room, the young man rekindled the brazier and slept near it until morning. He made a gift of wine to the giant, who was as pleased as he was amazed. At the front door of the house, the young man met the woman and gave her the silken kerchief, saying, "Dry your tears. Not every story here is a sad one. I have seen the master, and I did not die in the attempt." Then he made to leave.

"But if you have seen the master," the woman said, "then you have become a great lord and half the Empire is yours." She knelt. "If what you say is true, then I am to be your bride and Empress."

"I have never seen a woman more beautiful," said the young man, "but I am not a man of the Capital or any city. My life is on the sea. It is a hard life that would not suit you."

He left her. He followed the directions that the master of the house had given him. He recovered his little boat from beneath the dock, and he sailed home to his village. In time, he married a girl who had grown up nearby and they had children. In time, they grew old and had grandchildren. In time, they died.

Some say that the young man was a fool to turn down half the Empire.

Others say that if a mere fisherman had taken half the Empire, the other half would have gone to war against his rule and he would have come to ruin.

And a very few say that he had already possessed half the Empire before this story began, and that what he had refused was the *other* half. But the few who say this are strange. Very strange.

Chambers Like a Hive

IT'S NOT CLEAR HOW THIS began. He entered her life like smoke, becoming a little more solid, a little more real each time she saw him. She would find herself at a concert with him and not remember how she had come to be there. The first time this happened, he leaned toward her before the music started and said her name almost inaudibly, at the level of a whisper, as if someone overhearing could do her harm. This was her first hint of the nature of his spell.

As they waited in their velvet seats for the music to begin, he told her that in the country of his birth there was no border between the waking life and the life of dreams.

I wonder, she thought, if the dreams I've always thought of as light reflected from another world are only the light of *this* world, shining in another land? And she put the question to him.

He did not answer, but there were lights like candle flames in his black eyes.

The first chord sounded. She found she could not turn her head, could not free her gaze from his as the music rose and rushed over her like a wave.

Then, silence. For a long while she felt the quiet against her skin, a white resistance like cotton. She waited for applause, for the buzz of conversation, but no one in the seats around them even drew a breath. And all this while, his eyes were on her.

On the way from the concert, she would always hope to see someone she knew, someone she could call in the morning to confirm the existence of the hall, the music, the man she had been with. But this never happened.

She had a lot to learn. He told her that the night was a black lake shining with stars. Daylight was a white stone that the waters swallowed up.

She did not know if she should tell someone about him, if perhaps she should even ask for help. But what sort of help did she require?

Some nights she kept a vigil by the window, watching the clouds cross the moon, willing the coldness through the panes to keep her awake. On nights like those, he stayed away.

Only when she let her head fall, only when she grew light with sleep would he arrive with his gift of purple flowers and a word to wake her. They would walk through her house and he would discover for her all the hidden rooms with their painted-over windows. She had not known that they were there.

Are you the echo or the sound? she asked him. Where are you when you are not with me?

How completely he could shut her out when he refused to answer! How featureless he could make his face: a white slate.

One night, by gestures, he made her understand how many rooms there were beyond the ones that he had shown her. He took her hand and when she closed her eyes, she could see it: the maze of rooms and passageways that spiraled deep into the earth.

Ah, these are the secrets of my heart, she said.

No, he answered. These are the rooms of your house.

When he had gone, how could she not want to go there, to those cells and chambers clustered like a hive?

She did not wait for him. She pried the floorboards loose by day to find the passage, and as she worked she feared that without him she could not see the labyrinth beneath her bedroom. But when the last board was loose and lifted, there it was, the corridor, lit with a string of hanging bulbs just like a mine.

Should she descend alone? And whose place was this if not hers?

A long time she knelt looking, feeling the exhalations of cool air.

When next he came he seemed somehow diminished. His shoulders sloped and there was a rattle to his breath. Music? she asked him, thinking of the velvet seats, the hush of anticipation. He shook his head, lay at her feet, grew small.

She closed her eyes but did not dream. What if I say his name aloud, she wondered, in some crowded place where none can fail to hear?

Now, she bides her time. Beneath her bed the labyrinth unfolds and grows. Though he showed her to it, he doesn't guess that it is growing, could not imagine that she anticipates new rooms before they appear.

What does she owe him for the revelation? Would she have known to find these rooms if he had never come?

Each time that he arrives now, his clothes fall in deeper, blacker folds. When the music rises like a flood above their heads, it is his eyes that cannot leave hers. She imagines that she sees in his eyes the region of his birth: a plain and distant mountains. Nearby, black towers of uncounted rooms, rising toward a starless night.

She has guessed his name. It is a syllable always ready to burst from her. She keeps her jaw clamped tight against it.

He will grow thinner, until one night only his cloak arrives, rumpled at the foot of her bed. Still she will hold her tongue. She will take the cloak up, and she will put it on. She will never say his name.

Okra, Sorgum, Yam

SO THE FOLLOWING SUMMER when the second princess came to Old Kwaku's hut, he said, "What do *you* want?"

"My father said that I must learn wisdom from you."

"And is that what you want?"

"I wouldn't mind being wise, but when my sister returned from here last summer her hands were rough and red. She said she hadn't learned anything at all. What if I go home like that? What man will marry a princess who has a farmer's hands?"

"And if you must work to become wise?"

"I hope that you'll have better luck than with my sister, however you do it. Make me wise, and my father will be pleased. The he will marry me to a prince rich in goats and cattle. I'll dress in fine clothes and have twice as many servants as I have now."

"So it's wisdom you want?"

"Do I look like a girl who wastes her time? Yes, I want wisdom! Stop asking the same question and get on with it!"

So Old Kwaku, he told her what he had told her sister, that she must work with him in the fields all summer and through the harvest if she wanted to learn wisdom. She didn't like that idea one bit, but she couldn't go back to her father and say that she hadn't tried.

In his vegetable garden, Old Kwaku planted collard and okra and cowpeas. He showed the second princess how to cut the weeds down with a sharpened stick.

"I don't think I'm learning any wisdom," she said. "And look at my hands! Imagine what they'll look like at the end of the summer!"

"Here is part of wisdom," Old Kwaku said, and he began to rearrange some okra pods while they were still on their mother plants. He pulled one and nudged another and coaxed a third. He moved this one and that one together and tied the pods together in the shape of a little green person.

"That doesn't look like wisdom to me," the princess said. "Oh, I'm going to go home and die in my father's house, an old maid!"

Elsewhere, Old Kwaku had planted sorghum. He gave the princess a strip of cloth to wave to scare the birds away from the ripening grain.

"This cloth is rough," she said. "When I am married to a rich man, I hope that nothing this coarse will ever touch my skin! I will lie in the shade while other people work, when wisdom has made me into an excellent bride."

"Here is part of wisdom," Old Kwaku told her, and he began to bend this plant gently toward that one and to tie some of the seed heads together. Torso, arms, legs, and head. He tied the sorghum into the shape of a person.

"That doesn't look like wisdom to me," she said. "I hope I start seeing soon what this has to do with wisdom."

In another place, Old Kwaku grew yams. He showed the princess how to clear the weeds and grasses away from the vines, and then he had her dig very carefully to expose some of the tubers without damaging them. He had her pour water from an earthen jar to wash the yams while they were still in the ground.

She stood up and flung mud from her fingers. "Digging in the dirt is no way to learn wisdom! You're taking advantage of me!

Show me some wisdom right now!"

"Here is part of wisdom," Old Kwaku said. Gently, he moved the yams without pulling them free. He positioned two to be the arms, two to be the legs, one for the trunk and one for the head. Sure enough, he had put yams together in the shape of a person. He gently pushed the soil back over them.

"That doesn't look like wisdom to me," said the princess. "I should break that water jar over your head!" She stomped off to the river to wash her hands.

When it was time, Old Kwaku harvested the crops, all except for the figures made of okra, sorghum, and yams. He made a great big pot of stew, but he did not taste it and he did not let the princess have any, either. "Soon you'll return to your father, with wisdom or without," he told her. "We'll fast tonight. Beginning tomorrow, let us feast for three days and see whether, at the end, you are wise."

The princess didn't want to fast, but Old Kwaku slept by the pot with the ladle in his hand, like a guard with his spear. So the princess went to bed hungry for the first time in her life. When she woke up, she was very hungry indeed. Old Kwaku was already awake. He had set out three bowls on the mat. The princess knelt down before one, but Old Kwaku said, "We must wait for our guest."

Just then, a tiny voice called out, "I am here for now, but I'm afraid I'm not here for long!"

"Come in, come in," said Old Kwaku. "We were expecting you." He pulled aside the mat that covered his door, and in came a little green person made of okra. Old Kwaku filled the bowls and knelt before one.

As the princess reached for her bowl, the little okra person went to the third bowl and peered inside. "What if it's poisoned?"

The princess looked at her stew. Old Kwaku took a taste from his own bowl and said, "It's not poisoned."

"But how do we know," said the okra person, "that you didn't poison only mine? Or hers?"

"You saw me dish them out."

"Ah, but you're sly," said the okra person. "We weren't watching you carefully. And even if *you* are innocent, a witch might have poisoned it all while you slept."

The princess was very hungry, but now she sat looking at her stew without eating it.

"What do you care if you are poisoned in the morning?" asked Old Kwaku, eating some more of his stew. "You are going to die anyway when the sun goes down."

"Why did you have to remind me?" shouted the okra person in a voice so shrill that the princess had to cover her ears. "I don't want to die! Will I suffer? I don't want to be in pain! What is death, anyway? Is it only the beginning of more suffering? Poor me! I am going to a place of torment, I just know it! When will it happen? How high is the sun? How much time is left to me?" The little okra person cried and fretted and cried some more. The princess sat with her hands over her ears all day. Old Kwaku calmly finished his stew, then dumped the untouched servings of the princess and the okra person back into the pot.

When the sun touched the horizon, the okra person ran around in circles, shrieking in terror until it fell down dead. Old Kwaku threw its body into the fire and gave the princess the empty bowls. "Take these to the river and clean them," he said.

"First I want some stew," said the princess.

"No," said Old Kwaku. "Now we must fast until tomorrow. Then we will eat our fill."

The princess took the bowls to the river. She was very, very hungry now. But what if something like this happened again the next day? How could she eat with such a terrible visitor in the hut? What if she starved to death? She brought the clean bowls back and lay down to try to sleep, but she couldn't. She stayed up thinking about herself growing thinner and thinner.

In the morning, Old Kwaku set out three bowls again. The princess was both hungry and tired as she knelt before one. "We must wait for our guest," said Old Kwaku.

From outside, a little voice called, "I'm here for now, and I hope I'll be welcome!"

"Come in, come in," said Old Kwaku. "We were expecting you."

In danced a little brown and white person made of sorghum seeds. Old Kwaku filled three bowls.

As the princess reached for her bowl, the sorghum person said, "I hope this has tender meat in it!"

Meat sounded wonderful to the princess. She smiled at the thought.

"It's a vegetable stew," said Old Kwaku. He tasted his.

"Well I hope it tastes rich. I hope it's as smooth as butter."

The princess held her bowl, thinking of the wonderful taste of butter.

"It tastes as it tastes," said Old Kwaku, eating some more.

The princess was still very, very hungry, but the stew did not seem so appealing, now that she had tender meat and butter on her mind.

The sorghum person said, "Well, I hope we'll have something better tomorrow, something meaty and buttery that we can eat every day for the rest of our lives!"

"But you have only this day to live," said Old Kwaku.

"That's true," said the little sorghum person, beginning to dance around. "Oh, I hope I am going to paradise! I hope I have an easy death, and that in the land of the dead, there is goat meat cooked in milk. Plantains in honey would be tasty. I'd like to have some roasted beef. After I am gone, I hope I won't have to eat ordinary stews. I'll have fish curry with groundnuts!"

The princess forgot that she was holding a bowl of ordinary stew as she watched the little sorghum person dance and listened to it name all the fine things that it would eat in paradise. Old Kwaku finished his stew. When the sun touched the horizon, the sorghum person fell over dead, and Old Kwaku threw it onto the fire where it popped and crackled. He took the princess's bowl from her and dumped the stew back in the pot. He did the same with the third serving and sent the princess to the river to wash the empty bowls.

As she washed the bowls and brought them back, the princess hoped that tomorrow would be better. Hunger gnawed at her when she lay down on her mat. Old Kwaku slept by the pot as before. Perhaps he would fall asleep before she did and she could sneak a taste of stew. But weariness overcame even her hunger, and her eyes closed.

She awoke to the sound of a little voice shouting, "Let me in! I have no time to waste!" She opened her eyes to see that there were already three servings of stew on the mat. A little purple person made of yams entered the hut and stamped across the floor toward the bowls.

"You call this stew?" it said. "I deserve a better feast than this!"

The princess sat up and rubbed the sleep from her eyes. Old Kwaku picked up one of the bowls and began to eat. "It's very good," he said.

"Well, it's not good enough for the likes of me!" insisted the yam person. It tried to overturn one of the bowls, but it wasn't strong enough. "Why are your stupid bowls so heavy?" It kicked the side of the bowl.

"Calm down," said Old Kwaku. "Life is short."

"I know that life is short!" It kicked the bowl again. "I know it!"

The princess reached for one of the bowls, and the yam person said to Old Kwaku, "Aha! I see that you're up to your old tricks, deceiving girls and making them work your fields. Look at her hands!"

The princess looked at her callused hands and stopped reaching for the bowl.

"You got a season's work out of her, and what does she have to show for it? Her body is tired, her belly is empty, and is she wise? She's wise to *you*, maybe! Maybe she's finally catching on, you old fraud!"

The princess closed her hands into fists. She looked at Old Kwaku, who calmly ate his stew. She trembled. "It's true!" she said. "You're nothing but a cheat! I did everything you told me to do, and am I wise?" She seized one of the bowls.

"You are hungry," said Old Kwaku. "Have some stew."

"I'll give you stew!" she shouted. She hurled the bowl to the floor. She picked up the other bowl and broke that one as well. "You promised wisdom and gave me only grief! If I were a man, I would kill you!" On her way out, she tore the mat from the doorway and flung it to the ground.

"Are you going to let her talk to you like that?" the yam person demanded.

Old Kwaku went on eating.

"Those were good bowls!" said the yam person. "How dare she break those bowls!"

When he had eaten his fill, Old Kwaku cleaned up the mess of stew and broken pottery.

"Look! She didn't just rip your mat from the doorway! She tore the mat itself! Your best mat! Why aren't you getting mad? You let her walk all over you! I could just strangle you for being so soft!"

Using some reeds, Old Kwaku mended and rehung the mat. When the sun touched the horizon, the little yam person stamped on the ground, screamed with fury and died. Old Kwaku threw what was left of him onto the fire.

Now the next summer, when the third princess came to visit, it was an altogether different story.

The Beast

SOME PEOPLE TELLING THE story say that the beast looked like a jaguar, with claws and fangs. Others say it was more like a howler monkey, shaggy and upright. Still others say it looked nothing like either of those animals, that it was brilliantly colored like a bird and that like a bird, it sang. A few people say that the beast was plain and quiet like the capybara.

Then there's me. When I tell this story, I tell the truth: no one knows what the beast looked like. How could they know? All of this happened in the first days of the present sun, long, long ago, before the old temples were covered up by the jungle, before the old temples were even built.

A man had a beast that he had caught in a snare. He had never seen anything like it before, and he didn't know how to go about cooking it. Some animals are best roasted, but others are tough and need to be boiled. While he was deciding, he kept the beast tied to a stake outside of his hut.

It happened that the man's wife gave birth. Their baby came into the world with a flaw. His face was misshapen. His nose and upper lip were flattened together as if some power had struck him in the womb. He could hardly breathe. No doubt he would soon die.

In his grief the man took up a branch and began to beat the beast. Blow after blow fell on the animal until it collapsed. Then the beast raised its head and spoke. It said, "Take a little of my spittle. It is medicine."

The man was surprised that the beast could speak, and even more surprised that it should offer him a gift after he had used it so cruelly. But he went and got a little pottery jar, and holding the beast by the scruff in case it tried to bite him, he collected a few drops of saliva. He went back into his hut.

"What is that?" said his wife when she saw the jar.

"It is medicine."

"Who gave it to you?"

"The beast."

"How do you know the beast's medicine is not poison?"

"The child will die anyway, as he is now," the man said. He rubbed the beast's spittle on his son's broken face. In the morning, the child was healed.

The next day, the man said to the beast, "That was very good medicine. What do you want as a reward?"

"Offer me freedom and I will take it," said the beast.

"You are far too valuable to set free. But I will keep you in comfort."

"I cannot be kept in comfort," said the beast.

The man did his best to make the beast comfortable anyway. He built a spacious pen for it. He brought it many things from the jungle to see which ones it would eat. He asked it what more he could do as a reward, but the beast said only, "Offer me freedom and I will take it."

While the man was out hunting one day, he slipped between two fallen trees and broke his leg. It took him two days to drag himself home. His leg was black and greatly swollen. He suffered.

"What shall I do?" asked the man's wife.

"Get some spittle from the beast and rub it on my leg."

She did as he asked, but the next day, his leg was even more swollen. The man clawed at his own flesh in agony.

"Now what shall I do?" his wife asked.

The man tried to think. "Take a branch and beat the beast until it offers medicine."

Again, she did as he asked. This time, the spittle that the beast had given as medicine healed the man's leg. The next day, he was able to stand. "The beast must suffer to give its gift," he said. He made the pen much smaller and brought the beast only things it would eat when pained with hunger, not the things it preferred.

"Henceforth you will give medicine when we demand it."

"Yes," said the beast. "For now I am miserable."

"I would rather give you a reward," said the man.

"Give me my freedom and I will take it."

The man did not set the beast free. Whenever he or any of his family were sick or injured, they collected medicine from the poor beast and were cured. Word of the beast's medicine spread through the forest, and any time people were sick or injured, they would send a relative with a little jar. The relative would also bring a gift. For the man who had captured it, the beast was his family's treasure. The man and his wife lived to an old age. After they died, his son used the beast's power to keep himself and his daughters well. He, too, lived to a very old age. When he died, the beast passed to his oldest daughter, who took it to live with her husband. They built a tiny pen for the beast, as was the custom, and fed it things it did not much care to eat. They continued the custom of sharing the beast's medicine, as well as the custom of receiving gifts.

This woman and her husband had a son. To him, the most wondrous thing about the beast was not its medicine, but that it could talk. When his parents were not around, he went to the beast and said, "Tell me what are the things you like to eat."

"I suffer even to speak of them," said the beast, "for I have not tasted them in a long time."

The boy gathered up a great many things from the forest and give them to the beast. He noticed which foods it enjoyed most of all. Then he gathered more of those things whenever he could.

"Is that better?" he asked the beast.

The beast said only, "Give me my freedom and I will take it."

"My parents would make *me* suffer if I let you go."

"Only a little. I have suffered greatly for a long time."

"If I let you go, will you come back when we need medicine?"

"Give me my freedom," said the beast, "and I will take it."

Why the boy did what he did is a mystery. Once the beast was free, it might be impossible to catch again. Its medicine was a great treasure indeed. But the boy opened the beast's pen, and the beast disappeared into the jungle.

When the boy's mother and father found the pen open and the beast gone, they were furious. They looked long and hard for the beast, without success. When they were not searching for the beast, they beat the boy for his deed.

Word spread that the beast was free, and other people searched for it everywhere. Even people who lived too far away to have ever seen the beast now hunted the creature, though they often argued over what the beast looked like. How many legs did it walk upon? Were its teeth flat for grinding or sharp for piercing? Was it colorful or plain? Even people who had seen the beast disagreed. Not even the man and woman who had kept the beast could agree on every point.

The boy who had freed the beast died young of a fever.

In time, stories of the beast's appearance became more and more confused. As for the beast itself, other storytellers say it was never seen again. But how could anyone know, since people can't agree on what it looked like?

The One Who Conquers

ONCE UPON A TIME, some trolls lived deep inside the darkness of their caves. To feed themselves they crawled across the underground pools and streams, groping in the blackness for fish. When fish were scarce, the trolls clawed crumbs of glowing fungus from the cave walls or snatched spiders from their webs. They knew nothing of day or night, but when they were tired they pillowed their heads on stones and shivered themselves to sleep.

A voice came to the trolls in their dreams. "You are wretched creatures who do not even know your wretchedness. See now how other beings live." In their dreams, the trolls saw another world, a world of light much brighter than the glow of fungus. In this world lived creatures that, like trolls, walked upon two feet, but their ways were not at all the ways of trolls. They kept animals in pens, which made them easy to kill and eat. They made food grow up out of the ground in great abundance. When they were tired, they lay down in softness and warmth.

"What is this?" the trolls wondered in their sleep.

"This is the world of humans. The place you see is a town. The life you live now is hard and cold. I can give you this life that is soft and warm. Your bellies are empty. I can make them always full."

"Who are you?"

"I am The One Who Conquers. Accept me as your god, and we will take by force the life that I have shown you." Then he told them his secret name.

When the trolls awoke, they knew that they were wretched. They knew that they wanted to sleep in warmth and softness and to fill their bellies whenever they liked. So they built a mound of stones as a temple to The One Who Conquers, and they prayed to the god by his secret name.

Every night, The One Who Conquers came to them in dreams and showed them what they must do. They must leave their cave and enter the brightness. They must go a long way through a place where fungus grew hard and tall and across another place where fungus grew thin and no higher than a troll's knees. "Forest," said the voice in their dreams. "Field." They must find the town of the other two legged beings, kill them, and take over their lives.

"In the upper realm where it is all one great cavern, how will we find the town?"

"Say my secret name, and you will find it."

"How will we bear such brightness?" wondered the trolls.

"Say my secret name," the god told them, "and you will bear it."

"The creatures you show us are small, but you have shown us that they are good at killing. How will we defeat them?"

"Say my secret name, and I will protect you," said the voice in their dreams.

Awake, the trolls quarreled among themselves. They fought one another over fish, then complained that the fish were small. They groaned when they lay down on the hard cave floor to sleep.

"You are ready," said The One Who Conquers in their dreams. "It is time."

The trolls crept up from the depths of their cave. When they first emerged in the brightness, it wasn't so bright as they had feared. The roof of the one great cavern glittered with tiny lights.

"Where is the town?" they asked one another. "Which way do we go?" They milled about near the mouth of the cave until one of them remembered to call upon the god by his secret name.

"Follow my sign," said a voice. In one direction, they saw a green glow in the sky. They followed the glow into the place of trees.

As they made their way, the light began to change. A greater brightness overwhelmed the tiny lights. The sky grew fierce, brighter and brighter, stabbing their eyes. The trolls put their hands over their faces and wept until they remembered to call their god by his secret name. For a moment, green light glowed in their eyes.

"Open wide your eyes," said a voice. "Look about in the light of day."

The trolls looked about. They could see without pain, even where a brilliant light shone through to the forest floor. They continued through the forest, and out of the forest across the grassy plain, all the while following the green glow that shone even in the daylight.

They followed the glow to the first farms around the town. There, the trolls began to conquer, surprising men in their fields and women at their cook fires. The trolls conquered young and old. With their bare hands, they conquered cattle. They ate whatever they defeated. As night fell, the trolls crawled into feather beds or piles of straw. They slept in warmth and softness for the first time, bellies full.

"There is more, much more," promised The One Who Conquers. The trolls dreamed of full larders and even softer beds in the town.

In the morning, the trolls approaching the town heard the sound of a trumpet, which they had never heard before. They saw swords and bows and arrows, which they had seen only in dreams. A few arrows jumped into the sky, and one struck a troll. He howled and fell down, dying.

The trolls stopped. They fell back. More arrows flew.

Only then did the trolls remember to call upon The One Who Conquers. They said his secret name.

The green glow began to shine all over the bodies of the trolls. "At this hour, take this, my blessing," said a voice. "Go forward, quickly, without fear."

Just then an arrow struck a troll in the head, but it fell away as if it had struck a stone. A second arrow shattered against the shoulder of another troll. The One Who Conquers urged them on, and the trolls overran the town. In their eagerness, they knocked down walls, tore doors from their hinges, smashed barrels. They snapped the swords of the townsfolk with their hands. A few of the four-legged animals escaped from broken pens, but every one of the human beings was found and conquered before the glow had faded.

For many nights thereafter, the trolls feasted as they had feasted on the farms. Bellies full, they dozed through the days. In their dreams, they saw the town as it would be, with animals in their pens awaiting slaughter. Farmers plowed the fields and raised up grain. Blacksmiths repaired the broken swords and beat the crumpled trumpet round again. The town would be as it had been, but its people would be trolls. In dreams, the trolls learned to keep the fruits of conquest.

And so they did. The trolls lived the lives of the beings they had vanquished. They rounded up the cattle that had escaped. They rebuilt the walls, rehung the doors. They repaired the well in the town square and made the town their own.

The trolls did not forget The One Who Conquers. They tore down the town's old holy building and built a temple to their god in its place. They praised him above all other gods. They were rich, and on holy nights they gave over a portion of their riches as sacrifice to him and him alone.

They no longer heard the voice of their god in their dreams. They no longer dreamed together, never awoke from a single vision that all had shared. Even so, the trolls remembered him and honored him, their divine patron.

The trolls grew ever more comfortable, and stayed that way until the night when something half like a fish and half like a man heaved itself over the lip of the well and staggered across the square. It overturned a cart and tried to bite a troll who killed it with a sword. Then another such monster crawled out of the well. This one glowed green and the trolls broke their swords against it. When the trolls tried to shoot it, their arrows shattered and fell harmless on the cobblestones. More monsters crawled one after the other from the well. They, too, glowed green.

Trolls fought. Trolls died.

As they tried to save themselves, the trolls called out to their god. They said, "Help us!"

No voice answered them.

The monsters smashed walls. They reached their glowing arms into cellars where trolls were hiding.

Calling their god by his secret name, trolls said, "Help us! Why won't you help us?"

At last a voice answered them. It said, "I am The One Who Conquers."

Tiny Bells

SLEEPER, SLEEP WELL. Sleep until morning. And listen.

I am a dream. Once I was a man. Once I dreamed as you now dream, woke as you will awaken. I used to walk the world between earth and sky. Now I am a memory. If you wake to memories of a life you never lived, it is because you have let me enter your dreams. Threads of my life will be woven with your own.

Sleeper, I bring you a story. In the time of the Empire, the people of my village lived simply. We were happy. In our valley, we were at peace. The Emperor's armies were vast and we were his people.

People in the village of the next valley over were happy, too, as far as we could tell. Like us, they tended their flocks, sheared and traded wool. Like us, they planted wheat, ground flour, baked bread. For their feasts, they too roasted mutton.

But instead of proper houses, they built round huts, like mounds of stone. Instead of putting icons on their walls, they hung cut branches over their doors. The men tied bands of blue cloth on their heads, and the women wore metal bells on their wrists. They feasted much as we did on holy days, but for them, different days were holy.

We rarely met. From our farthest pastures, we saw them in their own farthest fields. In springtime, we sometimes passed them on the road to the market. When they spoke, we understood them, though some of their words were strange.

We had been separate like that for generations. We might have gone on, separate, for generations more if the Emperor and his army had not come to our mountains on their way to conquer the east. But come they did. More men than we had ever seen, men with swords and banners, camped on our hillsides. Their horses outnumbered our sheep. We saw the Emperor's square black tent in the distance. His general came among us, commanding the soldiers to carry off our biggest rams, to empty the fullest granaries. "Do not be afraid," he told us. "You are the Emperor's own people. We will leave enough to sustain you."

With the next dawn, the army was on the march again, over the pass into the next valley. At first, we did not think of the people there. We thought of the hard winter ahead, of the smaller harvest of wool for spring.

When we saw a great smoke, we knew from what distant fires it was rising. Then we did think of the other village. We remembered the general's words. "You are the Emperor's own people." When we took our flocks to our most distant pastures, we saw no other flocks, no other herders. I went into their valley. I saw the ruins of their round houses, the ashes of their granaries. Of the people themselves, there was no sign.

As the days grew short, though, those people came to us in dreams. My widowed mother dreamed of a woman her own age who was a widow also. My daughter dreamed of a little girl who wore bells on her wrist. In my own dreams I met a man whose favorite ram was black, like my own. In our dreams they said to us, "We are lost. We were driven from our homes and from this world. We are a memory only. Give us refuge. Give us a place here in your dreams."

Had they come to us alive, strangers fleeing before soldiers, we would have turned them away. They were not like us. We built our houses square and true. Icons blessed us from our walls. We spoke the Emperor's own tongue, feasted on the proper holy days.

But they came one by one, an old man to an old man so that they both remembered the same droughts and floods. They came one by one, a young mother to a young mother so that they knew the same weariness of waking throughout the night, and the same joy. They came one by one, a child as another child's playmate.

In dreams, I tended my flocks with the man who had a black ram. He taught me a song that I remembered when I awoke, and I sang it as I took my flock to pasture under the waking sun. In dreams, my daughter learned a game that she played with the other children when their chores were done. In dreams, my wife learned to make a yellow tea that she poured when I returned hungry and tired. It was good. I sang her the song, explained the words that were strange. Some of them she already knew.

Asleep, I asked the man why he hung a green branch over his door. Asleep, I asked him how he dyed wool blue. Asleep, I asked him who the traders were who would trade for tiny bells. My daughter wanted some to tie at her wrist.

In the spring, our village smelled sweeter for the branches over our doors. In the summer, our daughters jingled wherever they went.

The Emperor's campaign in the east was long. When the soldiers finally returned to our valley, there were not so many of them as before. They looked harder and bigger. Their general rode among us. He told the men to take everything—every lamb, every grain of wheat.

"But we are the Emperor's own people!" we said.

"Are you indeed?" said the general, and the way he shaped the words was strange in our ears.

We brought icons from our houses to show him.

Soldiers lit torches from our cook fires.

I tore the green branch from my house and flung it to the ground. Women wept and clawed at the bells on their daughters' wrists. The general drew his sword. The soldiers drew theirs.

Sleeper, I am a dream. Once I dreamed as you now dream, woke as you will awaken. Now I am a shadow of memory — your memory, if you will give me refuge. And here is my brother, who once tended a flock as I tended mine, who had a black ram, who was a stranger to me, but no longer. We were driven from our homes and from this world. Take us in. Give us a place here in your dreams.

The Dead Boy At Your Window

IN A DISTANT COUNTRY WHERE the towns had improbable names, a woman looked upon the unmoving form of her newborn baby and refused to see what the midwife saw. This was her son. She had brought him forth in agony, and now he must suck. She pressed his lips to her breast.

"But he is dead!" said the midwife.

"No," his mother lied. "I felt him suck just now." Her lie was as milk to the baby, who really was dead but who now opened his dead eyes and began to kick his dead legs. "There, do you see?" And she made the midwife call the father in to know his son.

The dead boy never did suck at his mother's breast. He sipped no water, never took food of any kind, so of course he never grew. But his father, who was handy with all things mechanical, built a rack for stretching him so that, year by year, he could be as tall as the other children.

When he had seen six winters, his parents sent him to school. Though he was as tall as the other students, the dead boy was strange to look upon. His bald head was almost the right size, but the rest of him was thin as a piece of leather and dry as a stick. He tried to make up for his ugliness with diligence, and every night he

177

was up late practicing his letters and numbers.

His voice was like the rasping of dry leaves. Because it was so hard to hear him, the teacher made all the other students hold their breaths when he gave an answer. She called on him often, and he was always right.

Naturally, the other children despised him. The bullies sometimes waited for him after school, but beating him, even with sticks, did him no harm. He wouldn't even cry out.

One windy day, the bullies stole a ball of twine from their teacher's desk, and after school, they held the dead boy on the ground with his arms out so that he took the shape of a cross. They ran a stick in through his left shirt sleeve and out through the right. They stretched his shirt tails down to his ankles, tied everything in place, fastened the ball of twine to a buttonhole, and launched him. To their delight, the dead boy made an excellent kite. It only added to their pleasure to see that owing to the weight of his head, he flew upside down.

When they were bored with watching the dead boy fly, they let go of the string. The dead boy did not drift back to earth, as any ordinary kite would do. He glided. He could steer a little, though he was mostly at the mercy of the winds. And he could not come down. Indeed, the wind blew him higher and higher.

The sun set, and still the dead boy rode the wind. The moon rose and by its glow he saw the fields and forests drifting by. He saw mountain ranges pass beneath him, and oceans and continents. At last the winds gentled, then ceased, and he glided down to the ground in a strange country. The ground was bare. The moon and stars had vanished from the sky. The air seemed gray and shrouded. The dead boy leaned to one side and shook himself until the stick fell from his shirt. He wound up the twine that had trailed behind him and waited for the sun to rise. Hour after long hour, there was only the same grayness. So he began to wander.

He encountered a man who looked much like himself, a bald head atop leathery limbs. "Where am I?" the dead boy asked.

The man looked at the grayness all around. "Where?" the man said. His voice, like the dead boy's, sounded like the whisper of dead leaves stirring.

A woman emerged from the grayness. Her head was bald, too, and her body dried out. "This!" she rasped, touching the dead boy's shirt. "I remember this!" She tugged on the dead boy's sleeve. "I had a thing like this!"

"Clothes?" said the dead boy.

"Clothes!" the woman cried. "That's what it is called!"

More shriveled people came out of the grayness. They crowded close to see the strange dead boy who wore clothes. Now the dead boy knew where he was. "This is the land of the dead."

"Why do you have clothes?" asked the dead woman. "We came here with nothing! Why do you have clothes?"

"I have always been dead," said the dead boy, "but I spent six years among the living."

"Six years!" said one of the dead. "And you have only just now come to us?"

"Did you know my wife?" asked a dead man. "Is she still among the living?"

"Give me news of my son!"

"What about my sister?"

The dead people crowded closer.

The dead boy said, "What is your sister's name?" But the dead could not remember the names of their loved ones. They did not even remember their own names. Likewise, the names of the places where they had lived, the numbers given to their years, the manners or fashions of their times, all of these they had forgotten.

"Well," said the dead boy, "in the town where I was born, there was a widow. Maybe she was your wife. I knew a boy whose mother had died, and an old woman who might have been your sister."

"Are you going back?"

"Of course not," said another dead person. "No one ever goes back."

"I think I might," the dead boy said. He explained about his flying. "When next the wind blows...."

"The wind never blows here," said a man so newly dead that he remembered wind.

"Then you could run with my string."

"Would that work?"

"Take a message to my husband!" said a dead woman.

"Tell my wife that I miss her!" said a dead man.

"Let my sister know I haven't forgotten her!"

"Say to my lover that I love him still!"

They gave him their messages, not knowing whether or not their loved ones were themselves long dead. Indeed, dead lovers might well be standing next to one another in the land of the dead, giving messages for each other to the dead boy. Still, he memorized them all. Then the dead put the stick back inside his shirt sleeves, tied everything in place, and unwound his string. Running as fast as their leathery legs could manage, they pulled the dead boy back into the sky, let go of the string, and watched with their dead eyes as he glided away.

He glided a long time over the gray stillness of death until at last a puff of wind blew him higher, until a breath of wind took him higher still, until a gust of wind carried him up above the grayness to where he could see the moon and the stars. Below he saw moonlight reflected in the ocean. In the distance rose mountain peaks. The dead boy came to earth in a little village. He knew no one here, but he went to the first house he came to and rapped on the bedroom shutters. To the woman who answered, he said, "A message from the land of the dead," and gave her one of the messages. The woman wept, and gave him a message in return.

House by house, he delivered the messages. House by house, he collected messages for the dead. In the morning, he found some boys to fly him, to give him back to the wind's mercy so he could carry these new messages back to the land of the dead.

So it has been ever since. On any night, head full of messages, he may rap upon any window to remind someone — to remind you, perhaps — of love that outlives memory, of love that needs no names.

V. Symmetrinas

Something Like the Sound
of the Wind in Trees

1. White noise

I'm not sure. Maybe it was the sound of sand hissing against the windowpane. Maybe it was tires on a wet road. Maybe it was the sound of paper tearing. Maybe it was the sound of water almost boiling. It might have been a distant river or the sound you hear in a seashell or a jar: the sound of space contained.

2. When the Phone Rings at Three in the Morning

You wake up with your heart hammering away, but your jaw and tongue are still numb with sleep. You say hello, but there's nothing there. Well, there's something. There's the hiss of the wires. You say hello again. Hello? Hello? But with your tongue so sluggish, it's coming out instead as hollow, hollow? That sound of an empty line, the hiss and buzz and occasional crackle, is more empty than silence would be. More absent. You fumble the receiver into its cradle, and a moment later, the phone rings again. Still, no one. Very insistently, no one.

3. The Ovation Lasted a Long Time

After the second encore, the musicians had left the stage, returned, gone away again, returned, and exited for the last time. But the applause did not die down. Finally, one by one, the members of the audience grew tired of clapping and stood to leave, but the sound of the ovation still hung in the air. Even when the last person had left the auditorium, the sound persisted like the rush of a waterfall. It remained when the building manager went home, it had not diminished when he unlocked the place in the morning, and it was still there even when another ensemble arrived that afternoon to rehearse. Perhaps, the building manager told these musicians hopefully, the sound would die down by the time of their performance. But it did not. Their music sounded thin and gauzy through the echo of the previous night's applause. Many in the audience demanded their money back. When the manager cancelled the next two performances and hired a team of acoustical engineers, they installed foam- rubber baffles and hung strips of carpet from the walls. These measures seemed to dull the enthusiasm of the applause somewhat, but they could not erase or absorb the sound completely. The place was now useless as an auditorium. The season was canceled, the front doors boarded up. For a time the building was vacant. Finally, the owners converted it into a warehouse. The fork-lift operators complained about the relentless ovation as well as the sloping floors, and they frequently went on strike. Even so, storing dry goods made more money for the owners than the music ever had.

4. Caribbean

In the parking garage, April fell asleep in her car, dreaming of islands with white beaches. Her engine ran. Carbon monoxide crept around the door cracks, slithered in through the ventilation. She kept sleeping. The gas was colorless and bland. It had no sound of its own, but it borrowed the sound of the ventilation fans, the sound of the sleeper breathing. In her dream, April felt the sea breeze in her hair. Her arms and legs grew heavy with sunlight. The waves rushed ashore, one after another, turning to foam with a hush, hush, hush.

5. She Wasn't There When It Happened

Sheila's lover, Ben, died of a heart attack in the street in front of their apartment. It was the old coat he wore that killed him. When he slumped against the side of a parked car, no one would help him. They thought he was a bum.

Sheila wasn't there when it happened, but she could imagine how it must have been: Ben curling forward, his hand reaching out of the coat's frayed sleeve, strangers shifting their gazes so that they could step around him without seeing him.

She tried to get on with things at work. She sent Ben's things to his family. In short, she held together.

Once, passing the spot where Ben had died, she heard a sound like the whisper of leaves in the wind. But there weren't any leaves.

It's nothing, she told herself. She went in, made dinner, and switched on the television. But in the morning, the sound was there again. She heard it on the street, in the subway, at work.

She tried to ignore it. She tried to pretend that the louder and louder hiss didn't exist, even though at work she had to ask people to repeat things.

The next morning, in the subway car, the sound intensified until it was like strong wind in her ears. Sheila looked up and saw flecks of light dancing across the faces of the passengers. It was as though silver confetti were falling right in front of them, glittering. As she watched, the confetti fell faster and thicker until the faces of those around her were like television screens tuned to an empty channel. She stared.

She missed her stop. She rode to the end of the line, where people suddenly had their faces back, and the sound fell off to a whisper. Because she didn't know what else to do, she went to work, but she spent the day avoiding people.

On the walk from the subway to her apartment that night, she came to the place on the sidewalk where Ben had died. The sound had stopped. There was no rustle or whisper or hiss. There were just the street sounds, shoes scraping the sidewalk around her, cars passing.

Sheila was too tired to take another step. Her knees felt weak, and her eyes burned. A sound started out of her. Her shoulders shook.

On either side, people shifted their gazes half a degree so that they could step around her without seeing her.

6. Insomnia Cure

When his parents fought, Walter would turn on the old record player in his room and drop the needle on the empty spot after the last song. *Psshhhhhhhhhhhhhhhhhh-pop*, it went. If he could still hear their voices, he would turn up the volume:

PSSHHHHHHHHHHHHHHHHH-POP.
PSSHHHHHHHHHHHHHHHHH-POP.

Filling the room up with the absence of music.

Thirty years later, after his own divorce, he keeps a record player in his room. Some nights, the absence of music at full volume is the only thing that will get him to sleep.

7. The Ultimate Mood Maker

In the new house, Jerry had trouble sleeping. As he stared at the dark ceiling, listening to Carla breathe, there were things that weighed on him: The job at the planner's office that had once been his dream and was now drudgery. The mortgage, which meant— even with Carla's income—that he needed to keep the job. Carla's difficulty conceiving. What if they kept trying and she didn't get pregnant? And what if she did? Worst of all was the thought of not getting enough sleep, of what it would do to him the next day. His fear of insomnia sometimes kept him awake all night.

The recorded sailboat sounds were Carla's idea. "The house is too quiet, that's the problem." She bought the recording from a mail-order company called The Ultimate Mood Maker. They specialized in recorded waterfalls, rivers, cornfields, and rain forests—she could have bought a whole library of restful sounds. But she bought just the sailboat.

It worked wonderfully at first. With the stereophonic waves breaking on the bow, with the gentle purling of the wake astern, with the occasional luffing of the sails and the creaking of the mast, Jerry felt the whole house gently rocking him, carrying him away to a place where the job and the mortgage and his insomnia just didn't matter.

But after fifty minutes, the recording would end and Jerry would be wide awake, staring at the ceiling, wondering if maybe he should have chosen an adjustable interest rate. After a while, he'd get out of bed, start the recording again, return to bed, and drift off into another fifty minutes of sleep.

Carla's solution was to buy more copies of the recording and set the stereo for continuous play, and Jerry finally began to sleep through the night. In fact, he found the sound of the creaking decks and splashing waves so comforting that he began to leave the recording on all morning. On the days when he was the last to leave for work, he left it playing so that the sounds of the waves were the first thing he heard when he came home. Soon Carla, too, was leaving the sailboat sounds playing around the clock. With the sound always in the background, Jerry sometimes felt, even wide awake at the dinner table, that he could feel the house gently rocking.

There were hints of the coming transformation, but they were too subtle to be alarming. When a crust of salt repeatedly formed on the front doorknob during the day, Jerry thought it was curious, but not inexplicable. After all, it was winter, and there was plenty of salt about on the roads and sidewalks. When the air inside the house began to smell distinctly of kelp, well, that was surely just a case of suggestion, Jerry reasoned. If you hear the sound of a sailboat all night long and for much of the day, you begin to imagine the smell of the sea, just as the feeling that the house gently rocked on the waves was an illusion.

On the morning that Jerry opened the front door and saw, not his front walk, but blue waves stretching to the horizon, his feet had already started down a path that was no longer there. He stepped into the sea. The weight of his water-logged suit nearly pulled him under, but he managed to grab onto the rose trellis and pull himself back onto the front stoop.

For a long time he sat there, dripping, looking out at the sun-flecked waves. He should be worried, he knew. There were many things now to worry about. But the sound of the waves lapping gently against the aluminum siding, the sound of the house creaking as it turned slowly in the current, these comforted him almost beyond belief.

8. When You Let Your Head Slip Under the Water

It's been a tough day. Well, when was the last time you had a day that was easy? But for once you're taking care of yourself. For once you're up to your ears in hot bathwater, and you've taken the phone off the hook. You relax and let most of your head slip under the surface. The water has a sound to it, a warm, cottony, muffled sound. Eyes closed, you hear yourself breathing, but distantly. There are clicks and tappings in the building, things you don't ordinarily hear. Life in the womb must have been like this. This is the sound you came from. You stay until the water grows cold, and when you open your eyes, your knees surprise you like islands sighted after a year at sea.

9. White Noise

I think it was the sound of my grandfather's last breath amplified many times over. I think it was the sound of a gunshot played back at quarter speed. I think it was rain. I think it was the sound of swimmers dividing the water. I think it was the sound of wind in tall grass or the sound of a brush fire. It was the sound of three degrees Kelvin, the sound of snowfall, of ashes stirring, of smoke rising up on the cold air.

Dead White Guys

1. Fathers of Our Fathers

We see their faces on our money, in textbooks. Washington and Hamilton. Jefferson and Adams. We read their words, but their words can never be the men themselves. So we light blood candles and burn gunpowder incense. We dance and chant over graves in Virginia and New York. "Fathers of our fathers," we say, "come forth. It's time to explain yourselves." We knock on crypts in Massachusetts. "Ours is a different time. Come among us now and let us judge you as men of this world and these years."

The generals of the revolution stir. Architects of the constitution wake. They put on new bodies and come forth. "Now we'll see who you really are," we say. "Knowing you, we will know ourselves at last."

2. Famous For the Wrong Reason

Who wants a write up in Sports Illustrated for a string of disappointments? The headline read, "Revere Comes Up Short Again."

But in this race you've been around the Atlanta oval almost five hundred times. Fuel tank dry, you're coasting into the last laps at a mere 125 miles per hour. But you will cross the line.

Coming out of a turn, thump, the car jolts. You spin into the wall.

"Paul," says your spotter's radio voice, "you okay?"

"I'm okay," you say, checking to see if you are. "What happened?"

"The number fourteen car hit you from the inside."

"I gave him room!"

"You did, Paul. You gave him room."

So you've extended your record. Despite great qualifying times, you haven't finished a race.

3. It's Who You Know

A woman hobbled into the Shoe Palace and slammed two shoe boxes onto the counter in front of Horatio Gates. "I want to speak to the manager," she said.

Gates stood tall. "Madame, you have that pleasure."

"You're the manager? The idiot who sold me these torture devices is the manager?"

"If you've found the shoes unsatisfactory," said Gates, "may I suggest that the flaw lies either in your feet or in your character. It could hardly be the shoes."

"They're too small! And I told you they were too small."

Frowning, Gates rang the bell on the counter. His teenaged assistant emerged from the stockroom. "Yes, sir?" said the boy.

"Kindly inform this person," said Gates, gesturing at the woman, "of the nature of this store."

"Shoe Palace sells only the best," the assistant recited.

"They don't fit!"

"Do you know the ultimate shoe horn?" asked Gates. "The ultimate shoe horn is a positive mental attitude. And I fear, Madame, that you are lacking in that department."

"Shoes have to fit!"

"And by force of will, they can be made to fit."

"How does a man who doesn't know the first thing about shoes get a job selling them?"

"He knows the owners," said the assistant.

"I would be qualified even if I did not."

"I want my money back!"

Gates laughed pleasantly. "If we gave a refund to every customer who wanted one, we could scarcely stay in business! I suggest that you adopt a more optimistic view."

4. Storm Chaser

Kathy drove the van. Ben checked the doppler radar. They watched the sky.

Twenty miles out, they could see what they had. Cumulonimbus clouds usually form towers. No towers rose at the edge of this storm. Instead, one enormous cauliflower blossomed from the center.

"Now that," said Ben Franklin, "is a supercell."

"I see it." At first, Kathy hadn't wanted to work with Ben. A grad student in his seventies? How serious could he be? But over the summer, he had mentioned things he had done, the English language newspaper in Moscow, the Amazon tourist boat, literacy campaigns in Detroit. He had hosted radio shows, written books.

All summer, he worked hard.

He wasn't all work, though. He flirted. Almost every fifty-something waitress in eastern Oklahoma knew Ben by now. Some seemed to know him well.

Drivers fleeing the storm flashed their lights. The sky closed.

"Hurry!" Ben urged.

Rain sheeted down. She had to slow. Then as suddenly as the rain had started, it let up. They could see.

A weak tornado dangles like a dirty string; a strong one looks like a funnel. This monster came grinding over the earth like an anvil.

Kathy stopped.

"Closer!" Ben said.

"Close enough!" She fought the wind to open her door. Ben joined her at the back of the van and helped her slide out the instrument package and lower it to the ground. "It's turning!" Ben yelled. "Perfect! We'll catch it right down the middle!" Kathy didn't look to see if he was right until she was back in the driver's seat, legs shaking.

Ben whooped as the van shot forward. In five minutes, they were safe.

"Shit!" Kathy pounded the wheel.

"What?"

"I've lived my whole life for that moment, and all I could think about was how scared I was!"

Ben laughed.

"It's not funny!"

"Your whole life! For that one moment! Really!" He chuckled some more.

Then she was laughing with him.

5. President of Baseball Operations

The secretary never had a chance to say, "Do you have an appointment?" Washington was already past her and opening the CEO's door. Benjamin Rush, the man behind the enormous desk, was on the phone. He looked up and said, "I'll call you back. Something's come up."

The secretary hovered in the doorway behind Washington, but Rush said, "It's all right. I'll see him."

Washington shut the door.

The CEO stood up and extended a hand. "Always good to see you, George."

Washington ignored the hand. "You've owned this team for

two months, and I haven't heard a word from you. Your assistant calls. You don't want an appointment, but your underling does. When I let a player go, I have the guts to do it in person."

Rush. "All right. I'll be straight with you. The team's been stuck in neutral—"

Washington looked at two glass encased baseballs on the desk. "Ruth and Williams. Any chance those are authentic?"

"They...of course they're authentic."

"How would you know? I ask because you seem to have a hard time recognizing the genuine article." Washington thumped his own chest with his fingers. "I am the genuine article. Did you know that I take batting practice with the team? At my age? Why do you think I do that?"

"George, it's not a question of your leadership—"

"Those guys would walk through fire for me. Hell, they have walked through fire. We were twenty-five games out of first place when we played the Yankees. Did you see that series? Did you see my guys lose in fourteen innings and then play their hearts out the next day to avoid the sweep?"

"When a team changes hands, some adjustments—"

"Yes. So here are the changes we're going to make. First, you're promoting me to president of baseball operations."

"Promoting you." Rush smiled a thin smile.

"But I'm still managing the team in the dugout, so I'll need to hire an assistant. Someone I trust. He's not in baseball any more, but Al Hamilton would be perfect."

"Alexander Hamilton?" Rush laughed. "He makes the kind of money I make!"

"He'll come down a peg for me. He will. Anyway, you're going to have to get used to spending. Pitching is going to cost us. Two top starters and a middle reliever. Then we're going to buy the best closer available. You're going to bid against the Yankees ownership until they blink."

Rush seemed to be fighting to keep a genial smile in place. "George, we're rebuilding."

"You're saying you don't expect to win."

"These things take time."

"We've got the bats, Rush. We don't have to go for the long ball. Singles. Men on base. Patient offense. Give me the pitching staff I want, and I'll bring you a pennant with the position players we already have. They'll walk through fire, but I want them walking through fire because there's something on the other side." He leaned over the desk. "So is there going to be something on the other side? Or is this a hobby for you?"

Rush's face reddened. "I want to win."

"But that's not enough. You've got to want to win as much as I want to win." Then Washington pushed at his dental work as if the bridge were loose. It wasn't, but the gesture would remind Rush that when Washington was a player, he'd stood in at the plate, bases loaded, and taken a brush-back pitch right in the mouth. He lost five teeth and won the game.

Washington reached across the desk, picked up the phone, and handed it to Rush. "Call publicity. Tell them about your new president of baseball operations."

And Benjamin Rush, to his lasting credit, made the call.

6. Madison of Madison Avenue

James Madison surveyed the conference table, the litter of scratch paper and chewed pencils. The waste basket in the corner overflowed with crumpled, rejected ideas. "There's got to be something here, something we've already thought of." he said. Then he looked at his watch. "It's going to be light outside soon, and we still don't have an idea we can run with."

Adams stood at the coffee maker, watching the carafe fill. "I love the smell of fresh coffee. It's somewhere between oak and chocolate." He inhaled. "Could we do something with smell?"

"New car smell has been done to death," said Madison. "Besides, this isn't just any car. This is the new Camaro. We're selling youth, nostalgia...something sexy. Where the devil did Jefferson get off to?"

"He had an idea. He said he needed to work on it alone. Coffee?"

"Heaven preserve me from another cup of coffee," Madison said. Then, "All right. Fill my mug. We have to stay sharp. Unless we dig deep and come up with something brilliant in the next..." He checked his watch again. "Six hours. We've got six hours to be brilliant, or we're going to lose this account."

Adams filled Madison's mug, brought it to him, and sat down. "I don't suppose we could say, 'The interior yields to your caress with the firm warmth of a young girl's breast'?"

Madison stared at him until Adams looked away.

"No," Adams said. "I don't suppose we could. But you must admit that it's youthful, nostalgic, sexy."

"It's not pithy, John. It lacks subtlety. Look, let's think in terms of argument some more. What are the reasons that someone would buy the competition? We list those reasons, then compose the advertising around counter-arguments."

"I don't suppose we could compare the wide wheel base to a woman's hips? A mature woman, I mean. Sturdiness and sensuality combined —"

The door flew open and Jefferson strode in waving a legal pad. "I've got it!"

"Great!" said Madison. "Let's hear it!"

Jefferson began to read: "When in the course of a lifetime of driving pleasure a driver enumerates those qualities which most contribute to satisfaction behind the wheel, he will...."

"Stop," said Madison. He looked at Adams. "When that comes out of your radio, do you or do you not change the station?"

"That's just preamble," Jefferson said. "Afterwards, the copy lists every positive attribute of the car. From horsepower and handling to the optional moon roof and CD changer..."

Madison rubbed his temples.

"I know what you're thinking, Jim, but I omitted nothing. It's all here. The Camaro is everything anyone could want in a car, and I prove it!"

"No," Madison said. "No, no, no. First of all, that's only every positive attribute you can think of. As soon as you begin to enumerate things, you begin to limit them! In spite of your best efforts, there will be people who will look at your list and will decide that just because you forgot to mention the cigarette lighter, the Camaro doesn't come with one."

Jefferson looked at his draft, then wrote something between the lines. "I mention the cigarette lighter," he said.

"What about all the reasons that people won't buy the Camaro?" Madison said. "You have to think about the immediate self-interest of the consumer. People are perverse. Give them half a chance, and they'll buy a Ford."

"He's right," Adams said. "There's a certain wicked impulse that inheres in all of humanity." From down the hall came the sound of a door opening and shutting.

Jefferson shook his head. "You're pessimists, both of you. I believe in the inherent goodness of every consumer."

A young man leaned in at the doorway. "What are you blokes doing here so early?"

Madison gritted his teeth. "So late, you mean." Paine was an intern from England, still wet behind the ears but convinced that he already knew all about what worked in American advertising. "We're working."

Paine looked over some of the scribbled notes on the table. "On the Camaro account? Oh, I have some good news about that. Had an idea of my own and faxed it to GM."

"You faxed a proposal?" said Jefferson.

"On our letterhead?" said Adams.

"Well, of course. I wanted them to take it seriously. The campaign is..." Paine gestured as if to an invisible marquee. "Bite the Night!"

"Bite the Night?" Madison pursed his lips. He stood up. He felt his face getting hot.

"Yeah, and the graphics that go with that are a leggy model taking a bite out of the moon as if it were an apple. There's a snake in a tree, and in the background, the Camaro."

"Bite the Night," said Adams. "You sent that to the client on our letterhead. Without asking."

"Another graphic could feature a good looking werewolf or vampire with a castle or forest. The car's always going to be in the background, in the shadows with the lights on."

Madison's temples throbbed. He fought to keep from shouting when he said, "'Bite the Night' doesn't even begin to make sense."

"Well, it's not really about making sense, is it?" Paine said. "It's all about getting the blood to pump. Anyway, they loved it. Called me up yesterday and asked to see mock-ups. Thought I'd come in early and get to work. Would have told you about it yesterday, but you were in a meeting." He looked at the three of them and once more at the table. "This meeting, apparently." He looked at Madison. "So I'm guessing you won't mind if I do up some art to show them?"

Madison sat down. "Use whatever you need."

"Cheers," said Paine.

When Paine had gone, Jefferson said, "Bite the Night. It does have a certain...something to it. Doesn't it?"

Madison glared at him.

Adams said, "Dear God. I have a feeling that we'll all be working for that boy one day."

Even more miserably, Madison said, "I have a feeling we won't be."

7. Give Me Amaranth!

Patrick Henry wasn't the first to think about amaranth. Some of his neighbors had put in a few rows between their corn and soybeans after the county extension agent had done a presentation at the grange. A big processing plant had opened in Danville. The market was new, but expanding. Folks were feeling the edges of amaranth.

No, Pat Henry wasn't the first to think about amaranth, but once he started, he couldn't let it go. In November, he went to Champaign to talk to some professors. He looked up recipes and just about drove his wife crazy, shooing her out of her own kitchen to try things out. He showed up at the Short Line Cafe with a platter of cookies and went from table to table.

"Taste the malt?" he said. "But there is no malt. That's amaranth!"

At an auction in Mahomet, Pat circulated with a seed company brochure in his back pocket, ready to tell anyone who would listen about how amaranth was really both a grain and a vegetable, depending on the variety. Some varieties might go both ways. You could harvest the early plants like spinach—only they had more calcium and iron than spinach. Amaranth was drought resistant and not particular about soil.

After he told someone all of this, Pat would hand over the brochure from his back pocket. A minute later, he'd have another one back there, tucked in casual like.

"Hey, Pat," folks said, "are you fronting for the seed company?"

He swore that he just loved amaranth. "Did you know it's loaded with lysine? Beta carotene? Vitamins C and E? It's high in fiber. The nutrients in a grain of amaranth are concentrated in a ring around the starch. That protects them during processing. Amaranth isn't just good nutrition in your field. It's good nutrition on the plate."

"Okay, Pat," folks admitted. "It's a good crop." Then they rolled their eyes when he wasn't looking.

Well, some did. But others were beginning to think that maybe he was on to something. When folks work their fields hard, have a decent harvest, and end the year worse off than they started it, they begin to wonder if they shouldn't try something new.

The kicker was Pat's local access cable TV show. In January, he taped "Give Me Amaranth!" He featured a table spread with packaged amaranth products. He interviewed the extension agent about crop yields and futures contracts for amaranth. He did a cooking demonstration with popped amaranth and interviewed a health food store owner. Local access programming was always on the lean side, so the show repeated three or four times a day through February, when those farmers who didn't have winter jobs in town had time on their hands. At the end of the month, they started ordering seeds.

Every spring, there's a sweet tension on the land. Farmers watch the sky, walk their fields, and wait for the ground to dry out enough to be worked. This might be the year, this might be the crop that turns things around. They plant, and in two weeks, green shoots have transformed the bare soil into something beautiful.

In farm after farm, all across the county, that something beautiful was amaranth. Everyone was growing it. Even the family living on the old Henry place.

As for Pat, he had moved to town by then.

Hail. Drought. A soggy spring. Early frost. A bumper crop in Asia that drives down prices. Some men can take the uncertainties of farming all their lives. Patrick Henry couldn't.

He manages the grocery store. Judging from what he stocks in health foods—the cookies, breakfast flakes, flour, pancake mix and crackers made at the plant in Danville—he's still crazy about amaranth.

8. Adams Consulting

In his study, John Adams sat writing a chapter about management theory. His phone rang.

"Adams Consulting."

"Hi, John. John Paul Jones checking in."

"What's up?" Adams checked his watch and wrote down the time. He billed by the minute.

"My supervisor is breathing down my neck. My programmers are months behind where they should be."

"And what are you thinking of doing about that?"

"I've called a meeting for this afternoon. I'm going to fire one of the programmers at random. As motivation."

Adams winced. He was glad that he did his corporate coaching over the phone so that Jones couldn't see that. "Okay," he said. "So let's hear your self-assessment. Industry over sloth?"

"Makes work for me. I'll have to hire a new programmer. Ninety-eight percent."

"Courage over compromise?"

"One hundred percent."

"Propriety over pleasure?"

"I still don't get that one. Can't something right be pleasurable, too?

"Of course. Married sex is one hundred percent. Sex with a mistress, zero."

"Well, I'll enjoy it, and it's the right thing to do," Jones said. "One hundred percent."

"John," said Adams. "Is it possible that the pleasure of firing programmers is counter productive? Do you think that the programmers who are left will likely feel that you did the proper thing?"

"What the hell do I care what they feel, as long as they —"

"John, that kind of thinking interferes with your professional advancement. If you're going to manage people, it does matter how they feel."

"Oh."

"You can't command loyalty out of fear."

"Sure you can!"

"Not for long. Now from that perspective, reassess again. Propriety over pleasure?"

"Hm. Maybe seventy-five percent."

Adams sighed. "John from where I sit, it's five percent." That was generous.

"Oh."

"Develop another strategy. Call me back."

There was a long silence. "All right." Then, "Adams, where did you learn this stuff?"

"I had my own coach."

"Who?"

"Get busy. Think about what you're going to do this afternoon."

As Adams set down the phone, someone knocked on the study door. It was Abby. She entered with tea and freshly baked cookies.

"Hello, my dear," Adams said.

"How's your morning?" she asked, pouring his tea.

"Good."

"Be specific," insisted his wife. "Industry over sloth?"

He smiled. "One hundred percent."

9. Headhunter

"Ethan? Benedict Arnold here. Is this a good time?"

"Hey, Benedict. I was about to call you."

"Can you talk?"

"I'm alone in my office with the door closed."

"Good. I'd like to suggest a change in timing. Could we hold off on your career move? For a month or two?"

"Motorola getting cold feet?"

"Not at all. Not at all. They want management talent, and

they're willing to pay for it."

"So why this call?"

"I'm jumping ship myself."

"The head hunter got head hunted?" Ethan laughed.

"Actually, no. I didn't get recruited away. I'm hanging out my own shingle."

"Ah. Now I see. If I go along and pretend that you landed me for Motorola after you were a free agent, then there must be some way for you walk with all of Motorola's fee instead of a mere commission, right? You are a piece of work."

Arnold said nothing.

"No offense intended," said Ethan. "We both swim with the sharks."

Arnold cleared his throat. "You'll wait?"

"To tell you the truth, Benedict, I may not take the Motorola job at all. Around here, I've made them understand what goes with me if I ever leave the company. They're scared. I can write my own ticket. My loyalty grows by the day."

"I thought we had an agreement."

"I thought you had a non-compete clause with your firm."

"They can sue me," said Benedict Arnold. "I'm going."

"And you can sue me," said Ethan Allen. "I'm staying put."

10. Hamilton Industries

You haven't told anyone where you were going. Coming alone at midnight to this parking garage to meet with Aaron Burr would not strike your friends and associates as a good idea. The union leader is ruthless. He takes everything personally. But you've had it up to here with him. He isn't pushing the workers to reject the latest offer because that's the best thing for them. He's manipulating the process for his own stature. And out of spite. It's hurting everyone. Workers need work, factories need workers. He needs to be made to understand that. Meeting in secret is an opportunity to talk sense into him. And if you can't, well, the garage is dark, deserted. A gun lies heavy in your coat pocket.

11. Parting Words

We relight our candles and say the names again. Franklin and Madison. Gates and Burr. Men who were bigger than their times and men who weren't big enough. We chant and dance our fathers' fathers back into the earth, into history. As they go, we aren't sure that we know ourselves any better than we did before. What was special about them, about their generation? What should we have learned? What is special about our generation, about us? Who are we? By the time we think to ask, it's almost too late. Only Jefferson and Washington remain.

Tom says, "Why ask us? Didn't we say that the world belongs to the living?"

George is more concrete. "Lean in at the plate," he says. "Lean in."

The Main Design That Shines Through Sky and Earth

1. For The Girls Who Have Everything

During the drive, Heather says, "Aunt Sylvie, what's for lunch?" She asks it just before we pass the last burger place, before the roads change from asphalt to gravel. She was along when I shopped for groceries: Oatmeal. Spaghetti. Rice.

I say, "Apples and cheese. Maybe a tomato. Want to split a tomato?"

"Okay." She watches the burger place go by.

I could afford to buy her a burger. By myself, I eat them whenever I want.

Another few miles of dirt road and sagebrush, and we're home. My house sits on ten acres of flat scrub. I have a bedroom, a sitting room, and a kitchen. I could have a bigger house somewhere else. But this is where Aunt Sylvie lives.

My sister has an enormous house with fourteen rooms, green lawns, and stables out back for the girls' horses. The girls take music classes, and gymnastics. They play soccer and softball. They have everything. *Everything*.

Heather helps me cut apples so thin that before we eat each slice we can hold it up to see the light shine through. When I share the tomato with her, she cuts her half into small bites to make it last. She knows that a weekend with me is a long time. Aunt Sylvie is boring. On these weekends, the only way to not go crazy is to do one thing at a time. Cut the tomato. Smell it. Taste this bite.

After lunch, there's nothing to do but watch the clouds.

2. First Day

It's your first day as a teacher, and all day, you're remembering. You show them the coat room. Today, no one has a coat to hang up. It's hot out. But you remember the red and blue reversible jacket you had and how you could stretch the tails out like a sail and lean into the wind. You believed you could fly, that you were always about to lift off.

The number one pencils haven't changed. You pass out the paper with solid and dotted lines for practicing letters. At the chalk board, you demonstrate writing the big O and the little o with a piece of chalk from a box that has never been opened before. Once, the smell of chalk dust was new.

As you go from pupil to pupil, correcting how each holds the pencil, you remember the smell of Mrs. Wolff, your teacher back then. She smelled like strawberry Koolaid. You think of those colors and flavors, the green green of lime, the red red of cherry, purple color that you never saw on a real grape any more than you ever tasted that flavor in anything but grape Koolaid and Jello and lollipops.

When your boys and girls say "One and one make two, one and two make three," you remember that you once knew the personalities of numerals: the aggressive 2, the mysterious 5, the happy 8. You remember that the child who made these memories — why should this be so startling? — was you.

3. Ms. Amante

Biology One is being team taught this year. One teacher is Mr. Tott. The other is Ms. Amante. Ms. Amante has long legs and wears boots that grip her calves. Her lipstick is the color of blood. Sometimes when she pauses and thinks of what to say next, she bites her lip. Her full, red lip.

During the unit on perception, Ms. Amante says that Helen Keller could tell one person from another by scent, and never mind perfumes. That's not what Ms. Amante is talking about. She means the clean scent of skin, and the students can smell it, too, if they try. She says that a man may fixate on the way a particular woman smells, may pine for her as he holds a sweater that retains her scent. That day, she's wearing a sweater.

There's something like spice and earth in the air on the days when it is Ms. Amante's turn to teach.

Ms. Amante says, during the unit on arthropods, that the male preying mantis doesn't know if he's going to get lucky, get eaten, or both. She says this with a smile that makes the boys wonder if Ms. Amante can read their minds.

Males compete. Red-winged blackbirds hurry north in the spring to scout locations the females will like. Big horn sheep make the mountains echo with the clash of horns. Deer lock antlers. Stallions rear and kick and bite. Some seagulls feed the females in courtship. Dinner first, then mating, says Ms. Amante. She says that humans like to pretend that biology somehow doesn't apply to them.

Her fingernails are as red as her lipstick. Her hips are wide.

All that effort to bond, and what's the result? Thirty percent of the chicks in a given nest are the offspring of another male, and it's not just mama birds that are stepping out. Rabbit, elk, and ground squirrel females slip away for something on the side, and maybe on the other side, too.

Ms. Amante is married. She never talks about her husband.

A certain hormone called oxytocin inspires the urge to cuddle. And other things. An ovulating mouse that gets an extra dose of oxytocin will work twice as hard to get males to mount her. As she reports this, Ms. Amante enunciates. Her mouth makes an O when she says mount.

The unit on vascular plants seems to be mostly about flowers. A male wasp sees the female of his dreams and copulates with her. Then he sees her sister—even better! —and has another go. But really, it's two orchids. The flowers have duped him twice. He's been taken advantage of, used up, and dropped off to walk the rest of the way home. And the students wonder, Does he mind? Such speculation is not officially part of the lesson plan. Ms. Amante won't answer the question.

Powdery anther. Sticky pistil. When Ms. Amante describes them, all the students, boys and girls alike, want to hear more, more, more.

4. Guru

Sam could have taken the number 15 bus. The stop was closer to his house, the route more direct. Walking two blocks out of his way for the 64 guaranteed that he'd be late, and being late could be one more thing that was wrong. One more thing in a long list. His house was a mess—dishes piled in the sink, floors that hadn't been swept in recent memory and probably had never been scrubbed since he and Cheryl had bought the place. The diaper pail stank. Cheryl's old cat had started peeing on the rug. Somebody ought to be taking care of all this, but Cheryl's hands were already full as she juggled all the things that had piled up during her maternity leave. Sam and Cheryl didn't have the money for a housekeeper on top of day care, not with the mortgage. On top of that, Sam worked for idiots. He didn't know anyone who didn't work for idiots, but his particular idiots were worse than most.

When the 64 arrived, the driver was some woman. Sam stood

on the bottom step and said, "Albert working today?"

"Yep," she said, "but he's got the other 64."

Sam said, "I'll wait."

It would cost him the fare of $2.50 plus another half an hour of waiting to ride Albert's bus, but as soon as Sam saw the driver's face, he knew it was going to be worth it. Albert was smiling at something a passenger had said as the bus doors opened. "Well, good morning!" Albert said.

"Hey, good morning," Sam said, paying the fare. The greeting was so warm and personal, but Sam doubted that Albert really remembered him. Sam had ridden with Albert only twice before.

"How are you?" the driver asked.

"Not so good," Sam told him. "Life's a mess."

"What kind of mess?" Albert said, still smiling. "What could life get to be, that you'd go calling it a mess?"

Sam told him: the house, the new baby, the idiot bosses.

"Well, sure!" Albert said. "But life is good. That baby, I bet he's beautiful."

"She."

"Aw, yes. Looks like her mother, don't she?"

"As a matter of fact, she does."

"Now," said Albert, "you tell me, sir. Did you marry an ugly woman or a pretty one? Did you love her on first sight, or did you have to force yourself?"

Sam laughed. "Sort of in between. I mean, I noticed Cheryl gradually. She's beautiful."

"I see. Beautiful wife, beautiful daughter. Nice house, too, I bet. A job that makes all this possible. What am I forgetting?"

Sam was smiling. He could have told himself all this, but coming from Albert, it had power.

"Oh, I know," Albert said. "You ever try washing a dish for pleasure? You make the sudsy water hot, and the rinse water cold.

Makes your hands tingle."

"Can't say I ever tried that."

"Sounds like you've got a whole house full of pleasure waiting for you every day," Albert said.

Other passengers, Albert's regular riders, nodded their heads.

In spite of arriving late, Sam had what passed for a pretty good day at work. He rode the 15 home and got dinner started. He played with his beautiful baby while Cheryl finished dinner. After dinner, he loaded the dishwasher and then scrubbed the kitchen floor with warm water. It didn't exactly make his hands tingle, but he found that if he was really paying attention to it, even scrubbing the floor could yield a sort of pleasure.

Cheryl had put the baby to bed, and then she had fallen asleep on the couch. Sam lay down next to her and stroked her hair. That Albert, he thought, knew things. The man was a guru of simple truths.

Albert, at the end of his shift, returned home weary. He had a beer to help him unwind. His face ached. It took something out of a man, being so damned sociable all day.

At the supper table, his boys were in high spirits, cracking wise. His wife told them gently to settle down. They didn't.

"You two cut it out," he warned.

They were quiet, but then one showed a mouthful of chewed peas to the other. They both laughed.

"Damn it!" Albert shouted. "Is a little peace and quiet in my own home too much to ask for? Go to your room! Both of you!" Then he threw down his napkin. It was already too late to enjoy his supper.

5. The Great Poem of Latvia

Foul weather began the misadventure which was to terminate in verse in a difficult tongue. The captain had hunted seals off the English and Spanish Maloons before, and he knew the islands thereabout, but in a heavy fall of snow and a swirling wind the island profiles were changed in their aspect. What seemed familiar was not, and the familiar lay hidden. Thus the captain, seeking safety on Swan Island, mistook some other rocks for a point that he must round for Chatham Harbor. He was confident of deep water, but the ship struck with great violence a ledge that was under the surface.

Under the American captain were four sailors: a free Negro from New York called Henry Dodge, two young Englishmen of excellent character called Joseph Matison and Richard Kenney, and the Spaniard Tomaso Limero who had signed articles in Montevideo when the ship needed to replace an American crewman who must be put ashore there for reasons of severe ill health. It was this particular composition of crew that doomed the ship, for as the captain perceived how he might save his vessel, badly stove as she was, so did Tomaso Limero have his own contradictory notions. Limero had always claimed to know these waters better than the captain himself, and in this moment of extremity he asserted his knowledge and insisted that he knew how to bring the ship at least to a place where she might be grounded and her stores salvaged for the survival of the crew.

For every order the captain gave, Limero interfered and gave a contradictory one. Matison took the captain's part and argued for discipline, whereupon Limero argued that the captain's orders were very foolish and should end in the extinction of all aboard. While these two nearly came to blows, Dodge and Kenney were thrown into a great confusion, obeying first this order and then the contradictory one. Either the captain or Limero might have prevailed as the ship's savior, but neither set of orders was carried to completion, and the ship soon took on so much water that she must be abandoned in haste.

They rowed the ship's boat through a growing storm, and for some time they followed an iron-bound shore where even if they succeeded in landing beneath the cliffs they could not haul the boat up and prevent her being dashed to pieces in the night. At last they espied a shelf that suited them, and they spent a wretched night soaked through, with the boat whelmed over on the rocks as their only shelter.

In the morning they sought the ship, but she had utterly foundered without trace. The men despaired of their continued existence. However, for their physical continuation they had tools that might serve even through winter if the men did not lose their wits. They had the boat for going among the islands, which the captain now recognized in clear weather. They had knives, some iron tools, and a quantity of cut saplings carried aboard the ship for the making of seal clubs. They had steel and flints for fire.

They at first killed sea-elephants only for their blubber, which served as fuel. In time, as they exhausted their hard tack, they began to eat the lean of those creatures. They also hunted seal and wild fowl. The birds of the Maloons were so unaccustomed to man that they might be killed rather easily by stoning, and foxes that made bold to raid the larder also made easy prey.

The shipwrecked crew built a shelter of stones. They dried the skins of fur seals, rubbed them soft, and sewed them with a sail needle and thread ravelled from the boat's sail. They roofed their shelter with fur seal skins, and fashioned Mockasins from the tougher skin of hair seals. When Macaroni penguins arrived and made a rookery among the albatross, the men feasted on eggs.

All of this bespeaks their efforts to remain strong of body, but the greatest danger was to their minds. For the short season when they might eat fresh penguin eggs, the men had brief respite from ordinary fare so vile it could be swallowed only with the sauce of immense hunger. The fox, rook, and seal flesh were often only half cooked over the spitting fires of blubber. The smoke of those fires made the skin of the five men all of one sooty color. When there was no blubber, fires made of dried Tushook grass were even smokier, more bitter, and less effective for roasting. Every day made the men more wretched.

The captain thought the circumstances of the wreck best forgotten as the matter now was of survival. Limero and Matison, however, regarded one another in enmity, and either one might erupt at any moment in insults for the other. By the light of a smoky fire one night, Matison beat Limero about the legs with a seal club and said that he would kill him for a mutineer. The captain intervened, but later Matison and Limero each sought out Kenney and Dodge to propose a murderous alliance. The captain ordered a truce but did not know what else he could do.

The next night, Henry Dodge began to mutter in rhyme. The words, as far as the others could tell, were nonsense, but when questioned, Dodge avered that they were a poem in the Latvian tongue. The poem was an epic of that nation, taught to Dodge by a sailor with whom the Negro had once shipped. And as he muttered, the other men grew restless to know the story of the poem. Dodge allowed as he could remember the story only in the Latvian tongue, but he would teach the words and their meaning to the men a few lines at a time, if they were agreeable.

Winter followed on with snows so heavy and deep that betimes there was nothing for the men to do but remain in their pinched shelter, chewing on the roots of Tushook grass and repeating lines of the heroic poem that Dodge taught. Now when disputes broke out, they were mild and about the poem, about how a particular line went. Dodge was a poor teacher as he often remembered a line in complete contradiction to how he had taught it only the day before. The men often remarked that Latvian was a queer tongue and took Dodge to task for his poor recollection of it. But through the winter, the poem grew more intelligible and satisfying to teacher and students alike, and the men took turns reciting it. Spring returned at long last, and a Nantucket whaler one day was seen and signaled with smoke, and the men were saved. Henry Dodge signed articles aboard that ship, and the other men were put ashore at such ports as suited them. None of them ever saw any of the others again.

The captain returned at length to sealing, taking pains to teach the men under his command a most strict obedience in nautical matters, and teaching them also the poem which gave him and many sailors under him a curious comfort in stormy seas. He learned only in his retirement and upon meeting a scholar from the city of Riga that the epic was only the most absolute nonsense in Latvian or any other language, which made the captain cease to teach it, but also to take all the more comfort and amusement in reciting it.

6. Legacy

Starting in her sophomore year, Karen tried three times to register for Dr. Laurel Black's section of EDU 455, Methods of Secondary Instruction. The closest she got was the seventh spot on the waiting list, and that wasn't close at all. The few, the lucky few, who managed to get enrolled in Dr. Black's section were unlikely to drop and make room. So Karen had to take Methods from Dr. Ryerson instead.

Dr. Black's fans—and they were numerous among the education majors—insisted that ending up with Ryerson was just short of disaster. The man wasn't a bad teacher. But in Black's section, students got the skinny on how to thrive as a high school teacher.

"Like what?" Karen asked.

"Philosophy of teaching stuff," said one friend. "Questioning assumptions. Working the class, not the front office. Putting the student first. The real student, not the student you imagine."

Another friend told her, "You get all these great tricks from Black, like 'Don't commit to teaching for more than a year at a time.'"

"That's a great trick?"

"Yeah, because you don't want to get dragged under by things that haven't happened yet. Or won't happen. She says you've got to teach like an athlete. You've got to be ready to return the ball."

"What does that mean?"

"You'd have to take the class. A lot of what she says sounds weird out of context. Besides, she says that we have to process things for ourselves. Teach the student, not the subject."

The closest Karen ever got to Dr. Black was passing her in the hall. She wanted to stop her and say, "Give it to me in a sentence. What do I need to know?" But she didn't. In Ryerson's section, she got some good practice in teaching by lecture, demonstration, dialogue, and group discussion. She did not learn how to be ready to return the ball.

In her first year as a new teacher, Karen went to the principal. She said, "I don't like the memo."

"Which memo is that?"

"This business about submitting lesson plans two weeks in advance is a waste of my time and yours."

He considered her. His frown was a bit like one of her father's frowns. "Miss Garry, you're a first year teacher."

"Exactly. What will do me more good than writing out formal lesson plans is to have you observe my teaching more often. I'd appreciate the feedback."

His eyebrows went up. "I don't have time for extra observations."

"You can use the time that you would have spent reviewing my lesson plans."

"Everyone got the same memo. If you don't submit your lesson plans, I'll have to write a letter for your permanent file."

She thought, That's okay. I'm only committed to one year of teaching anyway. She said, "I have to do what's best for my students, and that means using my time well."

During her first term, she was observed once by a senior administrator, once by the principal, and once by a master teacher.

The senior administrator saw her give a demonstration. At the start of the class, she discharged ammonia gas in a beaker of phenolphthalein solution. The solution turned pink. Then she inflated a red toy balloon with ammonia gas and put the balloon in another beaker of the same solution. At first, the solution remained clear. Karen lectured on the states of matter. By the end of the hour, that solution in the second beaker had also turned pink. "We won't get to kinetic theory for two more weeks," she said, "but in the meantime I want you to come up with at least three possible explanations for why this solution turned pink and a method for testing each explanation."

Her written evaluation from the senior administrator noted that two weeks was too long for students to remain in suspense about a demonstration. He noted that a red balloon might serve to confuse some students and said that she should have used, say, a blue one. He also observed that state-wide exams stressed factual knowledge and that demonstrations took up valuable time.

Later, the master teacher observed a session where Karen opened with a dialogue about what happens to sugar in a glass of water, led the students in an experiment at their lab tables, then demonstrated Brownian motion with a beaker of water and a drop of food coloring. Karen closed with another dialogue to confirm what the students had learned. The master teacher offered a few concrete tips, but wrote that Karen "clearly knew what she was doing."

The principal's only written comment was that Miss Garry was not submitting her lesson plans in advance, as required.

Karen took all of this to mean that she was doing as Dr. Black would have advised, teaching the class and not the front office.

Karen corrected the lab books for spelling and grammar. One student complained that the class was chemistry, not English. "Do you think the world divides up the way that school does?" Karen asked him. "Do you think that the annual report of a car company can be badly written just because they aren't in the publishing business?" That didn't mollify him. His mother called Karen at home to complain about the unfair grading.

"All right," Karen announced to her class. "Anyone who brings a note from home excusing you from learning job skills in this class will be graded strictly according to test scores."

Two notes came in. One referred to her as the "teecher." The other was typed, grammatical, and spelled correctly. She honored them both, and supposed that this constituted returning the ball.

No one had ever told Karen that Dr. Black used dynamic equilibrium as a metaphor for the classroom, but Karen thought of it as the sort of thing that Dr. Black would have taught. It fit. Like the chemistry of a living cell, the class room was always shifting.

Walking was another good metaphor for teaching. A person walking on two legs is never perfectly balanced. The body is making constant adjustments. It's not balance that keeps us on our feet, but constant motion.

In Karen's second year, a student that she'd taught in the fall committed suicide late in the spring. He shot himself in the head on a Saturday night. Monday morning, the first period class wanted something that Karen wasn't trained to give them. So gave them what she had. She invited them to talk about the boy who had shot himself. They asked questions she couldn't answer.

Near the end of the hour, she went to the blackboard and wrote:

$$KNO_3 \quad C \quad S$$

"Gunpowder," she said. She explained that potassium nitrate's role was to provide oxygen for rapid combustion of the carbon and sulfur. Gunpowder didn't need air to burn. In a confined space, combustion would result in a very fast build up of pressure.

One girl said, "Why are you telling us this?"

"I don't know," Karen said. "It's the place where what happened touches on chemistry. And also, I think, because sometimes the best way to think through something that weighs on you is to really look at it, to see it from every angle."

Later, she wasn't sure if it had been the right thing to do. But it was what she had done. She had kept moving.

After that, she did her best to notice the students more, to really see each one every day. I like the new haircut. What's the T-shirt logo? Is that a band? Pink really is your color. It made a difference, she thought, though she couldn't be sure of exactly what the difference was. And two years later, there was another suicide. Like the first one, he was a boy who had been in her class before, but was not a current student.

She dreamed about this boy. She dreamed that she opened her front door, and there he was, soaking wet, standing in the rain. He said, "It's okay." She tried to speak. She couldn't. She could barely breathe. He said, "It's not okay, is it? It's not okay." She woke from the dream struggling for breath. At the end of the term, she committed herself to teaching for just one more year.

Because she committed herself to just one year at a time, she always knew how many years she had been teaching. In her eleventh year, one of her students would come to her morning class with alcohol on his breath or his pupils dilated. She told him he had a problem and that he should talk to her when he was ready to get treatment. Soon after that, he disappeared from school for three weeks, then called her at home. "I've screwed up everything," he said. "I don't know what to do." When she called his mother, the woman was drunk. Hell, no, her son didn't need rehab. He needed a kick in the ass now and then, but he was fine, and fuck you, anyway.

Karen drove the boy to a treatment center and got him admitted. Days later, she was in the principal's office answering the mother's charge that Karen was having sex with her son. "I don't care how necessary it was for you to drive him," the principal said. "You should have been smart enough to have someone else along. I don't believe her, but you've opened us up to a nuisance suit. You've got to think these things through!"

The boy wrote her a long grateful letter. She saved it. For one thing, she might need it for evidence in case the mother sobered up and still wanted to sue.

She won no awards for her teaching. Some students adored her. Some didn't. Every year, she decided again that teaching was important and that she wasn't bad at it, so committed herself to another two semesters.

In the midst of her twentieth year, one of her college classmates phoned her. "Have you heard that Laurel Black died? You were one of her students, weren't you?"

Karen was not technically entitled to a bereavement leave to attend the funeral of a favorite college professor, but the new principal was younger than she was. She persuaded him.

Dr. Black had retired to her childhood home town in Iowa. Karen rented a car at the Des Moines airport and drove for two hours along fields of stubble. Trees had lost their leaves. The sky was gray.

At the funeral home, she met Dr. Black's daughter, Elizabeth, who told Karen what a great, encouraging mother Laurel had been.

Karen told Elizabeth that Dr. Black had been a superb teacher as well. For the first two hours, Karen was the only visitor who was not family.

In death, Dr. Black looked smaller than Karen remembered her.

At the memorial service the next day, the minister recounted Laurel Black's great contributions to generation after generation of student teachers. There weren't many of those former students in attendance. The chapel was small, and half of the pews were empty. The minister invited friends and family to stand and offer remembrances.

Karen stood. She said, "There may be days where I don't think of Dr. Black in my classroom. But there aren't weeks. She shaped what I do. I hope I'm a good teacher. I think I am. That after twenty years I still care whether or not I'm good at what I do, that's something I owe to Dr. Black."

Afterwards, there was a reception where Karen offered her sympathies to the family. A man Karen's age approached and said, "I had her for Methods."

"You're a teacher?"

"Was. I got out after six years. But what she taught me touched on everything else I've done. Thank you for saying what you said. You spoke for a lot of us."

"I never got to thank her."

"When were you her student?"

Karen said, "I've never stopped being her student."

7. Curriculum Vitae

It was, from some perspectives, a brilliant career. When Lance Reed first joined the humanities faculty, the theater program was like the theater program at any other tiny, struggling liberal arts college. Each year they staged two productions with cheap costumes, unimaginative acting, and uninspired direction. A year after Reed had been teaching, the students were acting convincingly in four plays a year on well-designed inexpensive sets. Where before the audiences had always consisted of students, parents, and a few idealistic faculty, now word began to spread in town that the college's productions might be worth seeing.

Reed brought a kind of energy that his mid-western students had never encountered before. He talked about their bodies as their instruments. As he coached them in breath, posture, familiarity with the muscles of their bodies, he would touch them, men and women alike. He would stand close to shape and arrange them with his hands. "Breathe in so that your belly pushes against my palm. Yes, like that! Now tighten your buns. Good."

The first student he slept with was the young woman playing the title role in Hedda Gabler. Teresa kept the affair secret, but suffered for living two lives. Suffering, Reed told his students, was good for any actor, but especially young ones who had little experience with it. "Boleslavsky said that acting is the soul receiving its birth through art. Birth is painful. It is a struggle!"

Teresa's soul was born on that stage as she played Hedda. "Now I am burning your child, Thea! Burning it! Curly locks." Lance had all the power in their relationship. Teresa knew a lot about Hedda Gabler. The affair didn't last, but Teresa was the first of Reed's students to go on to a successful stage career.

Reed's romance with Alice added little to the staging of Oedipus Rex. The production was done in masks and relied on technique rather than method acting. That was Reed's downfall; he was attracted to Alice, who played Jocasta, without ever having seen her act from her own core. But the time he discovered how little she had to draw from, she was pregnant. He married her knowing that such a marriage was doomed. But he lived what he taught: that the artist suffers.

The Dean of Faculty was appalled by the marriage, but by then Reed was attracting serious grant money to the school, along with students who came specifically to study with him. Reed was warned, and then tenured.

A few years later, the junior who played Helena in Uncle Vanya was indiscrete. Jordan pledged her best friend to absolute secrecy, then told her about liaisons with Reed. In a week, almost everyone in the production knew. A freshman who disapproved of adultery on principle thus kept a prim, tight lid on her performance as Sonia. In the title role was a young man who had a crush on Jordan, and his speeches to Helen sometimes veered close to things he really did feel for the actress. Serebrakoff was played by a student who somehow missed the rumors, but who detected and responded to the tensions in the rest of the cast. In short, the entire ensemble was perfectly motivated. A reviewer came all the way from Minneapolis to see and write about the production.

In her senior year, Jordan played Lady Macbeth, Roxane, Katharina, and Sadie Thompson. All of these productions were emotionally charged for reasons that the audiences and the administration did not suspect. The acting and directing were consistently superb. Jordan graduated in the spring, Reed divorced his first wife in the summer, and the professor married his star pupil the following winter. Three of the students who had played opposite Jordan had some degree of success off Broadway, and one launched a modestly successful career in Hollywood.

Jordan Reed quit acting. She bore Lance two children, kept house, and did what she could to protect his reputation with the other faculty. It wasn't easy. For one thing, most faculty continued for many years to treat her like a student. For another, her husband continued to have sex with his pupils. Sometimes he was careful, though he wasn't as effective as a teacher or director then. Intrigues and jealousies were part of what made his stage spectacular.

The year that Hamlet closed out the academic year, Reed was coupling with the actress who played Gertrude—sometimes in her car and sometimes behind the locked door of the prop room where her dramatic, rhythmic outcries left no doubt as to what was happening. That Hamlet was, according to one reviewer, better than one that had been staged the previous summer at the state university using professional actors.

The next fall found a black-haired, dark-eyed junior playing both the roles of Lady Macbeth and Reed's dark, Scorpionic lover. She liked asking him to do things to her that both excited and shamed him, and his intensity as a teacher was that year at its peak. She went on to a successful Hollywood career, though Reed often said that she'd have found her way there as easily without him. She was made for Hollywood.

He was still brilliant for a good many years after that. The college was named among the top ten undergraduate acting schools in an issue of Stagecraft. The alumni pledged funds for a theater building. More students made their way to New York, Los Angeles, or regional theaters.

Professor Reed's decline was gradual. His hair grayed and thinned. Though he worked to keep himself trim and limber, no man can escape the wrinkles or the loss of muscle tone that change him, in the eyes of young women, from a dangerous and exciting father figure to a pathetic, horny old man. Even if his appeal had not waned, his sexual appetite diminished year by year. His own children grew up and became parents. Eventually, he could not look at his students without thinking of his grandchildren.

His teaching became rote, routine. "Breathe in so that your belly pushes against my palm." He could give instruction he always gave, but he wasn't igniting his own passions. He wasn't making his students burn with deep emotion. Jordan had stayed with him, knowing everything, and his life at home with her became more important as his teaching became less so.

He retired early. The administration named an endowed chair after him. They were pleased to have the benefit of his reputation without the risk of, well, his reputation.

The college hired two younger professors to replace him, a

woman and a man. Both came with excellent credentials as actors and teachers. The theater program continued to have the college's full support. Theater Arts was, after all, the shining star for a college that had never had much to offer beyond being small and local.

Professor Reed developed emphysema. He and his wife moved to Arizona for the sun and the air. Ten years after that, students at the college proposed a symposium in his honor.

Holding hands, Mr. and Mrs. Lance Reed sat in the darkened theater for a production of Uncle Vanya. The woman playing Helena could act, she could really act. More than that, she was breathtakingly beautiful. When she said to Astroff that line that could be such a disaster, "I am angry at you yet I will always remember you with pleasure," she made it true, complex, heartbreaking. Marvelous, Lance thought, squeezing his wife's hand. Marvelous girl. Marvelous teacher!

8. Little Monsters

In the classroom, she was the grownup, the person who was supposed to have the authority, but when she told the children what to do, they often ignored her. And what could she do? She couldn't hit them. It wasn't allowed. But if she sent them to the principal's office they would come back an hour later with smug smiles.

She asked the principal about his notions of discipline, but he would say only, "Send them to me." But she wanted to know, were the children actually punished? "Send them to me." Whatever he was doing, she told him, it didn't seem to change their behavior in the classroom. "Send them to me."

That wasn't the worst of it. The worst thing was that she couldn't quit, couldn't afford to go somewhere else. She was stuck in the middle of these wheat fields, stuck in this little town that all summer baked under a cloudless sky and all winter stiffened under a glaze of ice. After school sometimes she would get in her little car and drive toward the horizon. Not far. She'd have to go such a long way for the scenery to change. A long, long way.

The kind of words she was supposed to use on the children were of no use. "Bobby, we use our indoor voices in the classroom." He'd be shrieking again in a minute, baring his teeth if he weren't getting his way. "Jessica, what have I told you about pulling hair? Stop, do you hear me?" The girl would look at her with half-closed eyes and give a slight nod. Yes, Jessica had heard, not that hearing made a bit of difference.

So the teacher gave up on the kinds of words she was supposed to use. She couldn't call the children by the first names that occurred to her, the words that children weren't supposed to know, but she thought of other things to call them. Things that struck her as funny. She thought of things to say, things the children would pay attention to. The children were as loud and unruly as ever, but she could now and then distract them with the things she told them.

The principal called her into his office. He said, "Have you really called the children in your classroom 'hatchlings'?" She admitted that she had. "And you've told them that their mommies and daddies are not real mommies and daddies?" That's what she had told them. "Why would you say such things?" Because nothing else worked. Because they really were little monsters. Because she needed to get their attention, capture their imaginations somehow. "They're children," the principal said. She told him that she was desperate. "They're children." How could she keep this up, working every day with such creatures? "They're children."

Later, she drove away from town about as far as she ever drove. She got out of her car and stood in the hot sun. If she could just keep going, there was another life out there for her. Except there wasn't, because she never did just keep going.

Back in the classroom, she didn't change what she told the children. She elaborated on it. She told them that her job was to teach them to pass for human so that when they grew up and moved to the real world, no one would be able to tell that they were monsters, little flesh eating monsters. All the mommies and the daddies, the teacher, the principal, all the grownups in town were real people brainwashed into acting like mommies and daddies and teacher and principal. But the children weren't people at all.

The children liked this story.

The principal asked to see her again. "You have to stop this," he said, "or else measures will be taken." She wanted to know what kind of measures. "Measures will be taken." She dared him to fire her. Go ahead and try to find someone else who will teach these miserable creatures. "Measures will be taken," he said.

She got in her car and drove again, farther this time. She climbed the bumper, scrambled onto the hood and then the roof of the car. She looked toward the horizon to see if she could make out imperfections, places where the sky met the ground with the artificial perspective of a diorama painting. She didn't see any. She kept looking for a long time anyway, trying to make up her mind about which reality would be worse.

9. Mr. Tott

Biology One is being team taught this year. One teacher is Ms. Amante. The other is Mr. Tott. Mr. Tott's skin is thin and tight against his skull. His eyes are sunken. His suit coat droops and folds from his thin frame, as if there had once been more of him. When he pauses in a lesson, his breathing whistles in his chest.

For the unit on metabolism, Mr. Tott tells the class that fermentation sets its own limit on the life of yeast. Alcohol is poison. When Lord Nelson died at Trafalgar, his body was taken back to England in a barrel of rum. Mr. Tott wheezes and laughs at his own story.

Everything is food for something else. For every act of living, something else had to die if for no other reason than to get out of the way.

The classroom air is sterile, dry as a tomb on the days when it's Mr. Tott's turn to teach. His chalk strikes the blackboard with sharp taps, as if he were driving nails.

For the unit on cell division, Mr. Tott explains that there are immortal cells. How many students would like their cells to live forever? When some hands are raised, Mr. Tott tells the story of Henrietta Lack. She died in 1951, but her cancer cells have stayed young and healthy, thriving in the lab, even infecting other cell cultures. Yes, she's dead, but there are more living cells of Henrietta Lack today than there are of any other person in the world. He wheezes and laughs at that story, too.

It's all funny to Mr. Tott: predation, infestation, infection. He seems particularly fond of parasites. There is a worm that infests a kind of snail. The larval worms migrate into the snail's antennae, turn colors, and wriggle. The pain maddened snail climbs to the top of a stalk of grass where it waves in the breeze and the wriggling larvae in its flesh imitate a delicious caterpillar no bird can resist. When a bird eats the snail, the larvae continue to develop inside the bird, their second host. Sometimes when he laughs, Mr. Tott coughs and can't stop.

The prettiest little octopus is the one with deadly venom. A black mamba kills with neurotoxins while the victim, wide awake, can feel it happen, can wait for the next breath that he can't quite get his lungs to breathe. Pit viper venom digests as it kills with an efficiency that Mr. Tott calls elegant.

Evolution needs death, says Mr. Tott, every bit as much as it needs sex. What's it to be? Youthful trauma? Greedy cancers? A heart that starves? Stroke? Or the tiny, progressive breakdowns of cells that just get tired of dividing? He says that humans like to pretend that biology somehow doesn't apply to them.

In a whisper that everyone can hear, Mr. Tott explains his trinity: apoptosis, oncosis, and necrosis. He's just getting started, but the students have heard enough, enough, enough.

10. Stories

It's the end of your last day as a teacher. You have closed your office door and returned to your chair. Jerry Lavin, a junior, sits on the other side of your desk, alternately holding his breath to keep from sobbing, and sobbing anyway. His face is red and wet. On the last day of school, it's too warm for his letter jacket, but he has worn it anyway, as if being the star defensive back could protect him from the mess he has gotten himself into. Rosie Horne is pregnant, and Jerry tells you he has to do the right thing.

Has to. That tells you something. That hints at some possible outcomes.

You teach social studies—history—but you're also the teacher they come to with their stories, with what they think of as their happy or unhappy endings.

Jerry's a good kid. You taught his dad. You could tell Jerry a story or two about his old man, if you wanted.

For Rosie, marrying Jerry will be a step up for her. Did she know that? Calculate it?

What happens next?

There is so much that you won't miss about teaching. But these kids...which ones end up in college, dead, in jail, or working at the grocery? Now you're retiring, and you'll lose the thread of their stories. That's the thing that makes you take a deep breath, let it out.

Jerry Lavin takes a deep breath, too. He says thank you, thank you for listening.

11. Spanish Lesson

When I put the daisies on the window sill, my father said from his bed, "Aren't the flowers supposed to come after I'm gone?" There were already two bouquets on the dresser, another on the bed table.

"Better to get them while you're here to smell them," I said.

"Can't smell anything but plastic." He motioned toward the oxygen tube under his nose. Then he said, "Teach me Spanish."

I thought, *Why?* but said, "What do you want to learn?"

"Everything."

The doctor had said, *It's a matter of weeks or days, not months.*

"Okay." I taught him the difference between the permanent *ser* and the temporary *estar*.

Yo soy. Yo estoy.

The next day, I brought him the text that I used at school. We talked adjectives.

The day after that, the nurses told me that when he wasn't sleeping, he was sounding out words in the book.

"It's backwards," he declared. "*Me lo dió.* Why isn't it *Dió lo me?*"

"Because it's Spanish."

"And who decides what's feminine, what's masculine? *La flor,* okay. But *la guerra?* War is feminine?"

"*Guer-r-r-a,*" I said. "Trill the double r." He tried.

Three days later, I watched him sleep. He woke up, squinted. I wasn't sure, as his gaze wandered, if he knew who I was. He cleared his throat. "*Estoy rodeado por flores.*"

"*De flores,*" I corrected. "*Sí, papí. Estás rodeado de flores.* Flowers all around."

"I speak Spanish!"

We laughed. And that was it, the last laugh we had together.

Other books by

Bruce Holland Rogers

Thirteen Ways to Water

Flaming Arrows

Word Work

Printed in the United States
53249LVS00002B/280-297